D1244624

CLOUD NINE

CLOUD NINE

James M. Cain

THE MYSTERIOUS PRESS • NEW YORK

Library of Congress Catalogue Number: 83-63036
ISBN: 0-89296-079-5 Trade Edition

FIRST EDITION

Chapter 1

I first met her, this girl that I married a few days later, and that the papers have crucified under the pretense of glorification, on a Friday morning in June, on the parking lot by the Patuxent Building, that my office is in. It was around 9:30, and I was late getting in, on account of a call I'd had, from the buyer I had lined up for a house I'd signed on to sell, who had gone away unexpectedly and wired me to stand by. So I did, he called, and we closed, without even much of a haggle over the $65,000 I asked. As you can imagine, I was feeling pretty good, and whistled as I parked.

But then, when I got out of the car, this girl stepped up and spoke to me by name. She was a quite pretty girl, around eighteen as I thought, a cornhusk blonde with blue eyes, fair skin, and snubby nose, as well as a shape to write home about. She was no more than medium height, but beautifully formed in all departments. She was dressed as girls dress for church, not for school, play, or the supermarket, in dark blue silk, black hat, bag, and shoes. The dress showed plenty of leg, and yet wasn't too terribly short. "Yes?" I answered. "I'm Graham Kirby. What can I do for you?"

"Mr. Kirby, I'm Sonya Lang."

She said it as though I should know who Sonya Lang was, and I did have a vague impression I'd seen her somewhere before, but beyond that I didn't place her or her name. "Oh — ?" I said. "What is it, Miss Lang? Or perhaps you'd like to come to my office. It's right here in the building."

"Well — is there some other place we could talk?. . .I mean, it's why I waited here, waited until you came, so I would *not* have to go to your office. The business I have with you, it's better I not be seen there. I called in, to ask you to meet me somewhere, and when they said you'd be in directly, I walked over to wait for you."

It all seemed a bit odd, but in the real estate business, which involves the homes people live in, you get a wacky fallout, and don't pay too much attention. So I guess I was slightly impatient as I told her: "Miss Lang, I've a busy day ahead, and don't have much time to spare. It would help if you'd give me some idea what this is all about — ?"

"Okay, Mr. Graham Kirby, I will. I'm pregnant, that's what it's about, by your brother Burwell. I'm pregnant from him raping me, and I badly need your help. I need help on account of my family, on account of my father mostly, who's threatening things I'm afraid of, things that concern *you,* or should, Mr. Kirby — but before you can do anything, or know what you're *trying* to do, I'd have to explain to you, how things are with me. *Well do we have to talk here, Mr. Kirby? Where the whole street can hear us? Or —"*

"Please, Miss Lang! Please!"

My head was spinning, and I cut in with all kinds of stuff, to ease things off a bit and gain a minute to think — like saying how grateful I was, she had shown such discretion, in not going up to my office — virtually meaningless things like that. I'm not sure now, what I said. But then, when my bewilderment diminished, I told her, "We can go to my house, Miss Lang, where we'll have the place to ourselves and you'll be free to say anything. But will you give me a minute? To go up and clear my decks? So I'll be completely free? To talk—or whatever you want of me?"

"Okay. Sure."

"Would you care to wait in the car?"

"Yes, that'll be fine."

I put her in, and started around the front, headed for the sidewalk, which led to the building entrance, but then I thought: Wake up, get with it, didn't you hear what this girl said? Suppose you take too long, suppose she gets tired waiting, and takes a notion to blow? What then? You wouldn't know how to find her, and you can't know what she'd pull. A girl pregnant by your brother is not a minor problem. She's the first order of business on anyone's office calendar. I walked back to the car and got in behind the wheel. "I think we'll go now," I said. "I can call my office from home."

"Whatever you say, Mr. Kirby."

So we started out on our ten-minute drive, and on the way she had nothing to say and certainly I didn't. There was time enough, though, for cold rage to move in on me, at Burwell Stuart, for the trouble he'd been to me, and of course to his mother, who of course was also my mother. Actually, he wasn't my brother, but only my half brother, as my mother had married again, after my father died, and Burwell, or Burl as he was called, was the result. I suppose it was natural I didn't like him, as I hadn't liked his father, and in fact was horribly jolted, and not only jolted but ashamed, when my mother married him.

We had lived at Cabin John, on the Potomac above Washington, until I was eight and my father died. Then Harrison Stuart appeared on the scene, a big wheel in

Prince George County, which is east and south of Washington, not north of it as Montgomery County is, where Cabin John is located.

My stepfather was a former county commissioner, powerful in Democratic circles, as well as with the ladies. It was his activities with them that embittered me, from the rumors I heard everywhere. He and my mother had a hook-up, I would say, rather than a regular marriage, and she she may have known of his outside activities, yet not have wanted to joggle the combos he had, which at least he made pay—and big too. But I got along with him so badly that when a lady she knew, by the name of Mrs. Sibert, Mrs. Jane Sibert, offered to take me in and raise me on her farm, I got down on my knees to my mother and begged her to let me go.

So she did, and my pleasant years began—in high school, at Yale, and in real estate, which was the business my father had been in. But it wasn't the end of Burl. His father died when he was fifteen, but even before then, it was clear to all and sundry he would carry the old man's torch.

By the time he was twelve he'd been mixed up with two girls, and then when he was a senior in high school he raped a teacher. He carried her books home one day, and when she asked him in he upped her skirts and raped her. Next day she went boiling over to Mother, to say what she meant to do. But Mother wasn't home, and who opened the door was Burl. The second time around, she decided that being raped wasn't so bad, and it became a scandal in school. So after he graduated she quit, and when he did his hitch in the Army she followed him to Japan when he was stationed there for a while, and then followed him back. On his discharge, he now being twenty-one, it had seemed that they would get married, but then she got killed, when her car hit a culvert wall, with her mother at the wheel, as the two of them were on the way to Bowie, where her parents lived. So that was the end of her, but I heard there were other girls, so his mother never knew, from one week to the next, what to expect. So I was all sulked up, just from thinking about it, and perhaps to cover, to have something to say, perhaps to cool it a little, I asked, in a conversational way, "Sonya, how old are you?"

"I'm almost seventeen."

"Ouch."

"What's the matter, Mr. Kirby?"

"Nothing—I took you for older, that's all."

"You mean, when it happened, I was within the law."

"Yes, I guess that's what I mean—if you invoke the law. Sonya, I haven't heard the details, but have you really thought about it, what invoking the law means? It protects the girl, that's true, especially a girl under the age of consent, but she often finds out that its protection is just about the worst thing that can happen to her."

"It's not me. It's my family."

"Oh yes, you mentioned your father."

"How old are you, Mr. Kirby?"

"I was thirty last September."

"Now it's my turn to say ouch."

"Why, Sonya?"

"I took you for younger, that's all."

In spite of the butterflies I had in my stomach, you could even say blue-tail flies, I found myself liking this girl, and then a funny thing happened. When I pulled up in front of my house, several cars were there, as usual, with open spaces between. To slip into one of them, I pulled up next to a car, then did the usual parking maneuver: I angled toward the center of the street, then dropped back to catch my rear wheels on the curb. Then I pulled up and cut my front wheels, to throw my front end toward the curb. Then I backed and snugged into the open space, with front and rear wheels touching. But of course, half the time I was twisted around, to look out the rear window and see what I was doing.

That brought me facing her. But she twisted around too, and that brought her facing me. Her head touched my coat, and as it did I could swear she inhaled, as though sniffing what I smelled like.

Chapter 2

I live in College Heights Estates, in a big brick house painted white, with dark green shutters, dark green trees, and dark green grass. College Heights Estates is a swank development, but most of the places are hummocky. The houses stand on rolling ground, or have hills rising behind, or to one side or the other.

My place, though, is on the flat, and for that reason somewhat special. It has a center hall, with steps on one side leading up, powder room and coat closet across on the other side, and beyond the steps a partition, with a door that leads to a den—the kitchen, pantry, and storage area being beyond that. Just inside the front door, before the steps begin, is a wide entrance foyer, with arches on each side, the one on the right leading to the living room, the other to the dining room. Topside, on the second deck, is a master bedroom and three junior bedrooms, the master with its own private bath, the others with a bath off the hall.

It just suggests being a mansion, and I need it like I need

Buckingham Palace, but I got it in a trade, so cheap it was practically a gift, and I suppose vanity entered in: I couldn't resist living in it. So I said good-bye to Jane Sibert, bought furniture at the Plaza, and when it arrived moved in.

Once I got it organized, it cost less than you might think. I hired on a gardener, bought him a sit-on-it mower, and let him do his stuff. Also, I took on a cleaning woman, a character named Modesta, to make the bed every day and keep the place in order. Except for breakfast, which I made myself, I took my meals out, mostly at the Royal Arms, a pretty good place near the Plaza, where I practically became a boarder. All in all, at not too much expense, I lived quite stylishly.

I showed Sonya into the living room, saw vac tracks on the rug, and told her: "The cleaning woman's already been here, so we'll have the place to ourselves. If you'll give me a minute to call my office, I'll straighten some things out there, and then be free to hear what you have to tell me."

She said okay and I used the hall extension. Mabel, the switchboard girl, answered, and I had her give me Miss Musick, my secretary, and started it off very breezy: "Helen, something's come up, that may keep me till afternoon, but will you have Jack Kefoe call the owner of that Riverdale house, and tell him I sold it for him? At our advertised price? And will you ask him to call the lawyers and get them started doing their stuff? But he'll know about that." She could have called the owner, but I wanted Jack to do it, as he was the salesman assigned to the deal, and I wanted to reassure him that though I'd closed with the owner, it was still his sale, and that I wasn't cutting in. In my business you keep your salesmen happy, and especially you keep their confidence, so they know you're not playing them tricks.

Then I asked, "Has anything come up?" and she said my mother had called, twice. I said okay, I'd call her back.

When I asked, "Anything else?" she mentioned the proofs of our ads for the Sunday papers, which ordinarily are my special concern, but I told her: "Just check them against the copy, and if everything is in order, phone our release in." And then, "Anything else?"

"Yes, Mr. Kirby," she said, after a moment's hesitation. "A girl called, wanting to talk to you, and when I said you were out, she asked when you'd be in, and I told her we expected you any minute. She didn't leave her name, *but*—Mr. Kirby, she seemed upset and so did your mother. I had the feeling there's some connection, and that—*this girl means trouble.*"

"Fine, I'll duly get the shakes."

"Well you needn't laugh."

"I'll be on my guard against her."

Her habit of imagining things under my bed was kind of a joke between us, and I played it the way I would have, if the girl hadn't been right in my own living room. When I went in there, she was making the grand tour of the pictures I had on the walls, one or two paintings of ancestors Mother had, the rest were big color photos of houses I'd had something to do with, all hung above the bookcases that lined the room, which stopped at eye level.

She said, "I love your books, Mr. Kirby—and *that* house I've seen—and *that* one—and *that* one. They're beautiful, just beautiful." And then, "Was that me she was talking about?"

"Probably. She said a girl called in."

"What did she say about me?"

"That you mean trouble, she thought."

"She didn't know the half."

She laughed, and I asked, "Would you like a Coke?" But at that she bit her lip and it seemed she wanted to cry.

When I asked what the trouble was, she said, "It's what you say to a child—you know nothing else to say, but there she is, so you ask will she have a Coke. Suppose I said yes, what then?"

"I'd get you a Coke, that's all."

"Well, no thanks. I'm not a child!"

She did sob as she said that, and I began to get the picture, of how this girl could crack jokes, for a minute from force of habit, the kind of jokes young kids crack, and then remember the mess she was in, which wasn't a joke at all. I put my arms around her, patted her, and got my handkerchief out. After I'd wiped her eyes I let her blow her nose, which made her laugh again.

I sat her down and said, "Right, let's begin." The furniture's modern and full-size to go with the 30*x*18 room, upholstered in beige, in contrast with the rug, which is light maroon. But flanking the fireplace are sofas, with a cocktail table between, and I put her on one, taking the other myself, facing her. But facing her that way, as she sank back on the cushions, meant a perfect up-from-the-knees view of the most beautiful legs I'd ever seen, and they rang a bell—I knew I'd seen them before. She asked, "You want to hear it all? You want me to commence at the beginning?"

"Sure. Why not?"

"Then, I won't leave anything out."

But I was beginning to note how she talked, in the funny, left-handed way that Southern Maryland people have. She didn't say *anything,* she said *innything*. But all I said was: "Shoot!"

"Did you know Dale Morgan, Mr. Kirby?"

"The teacher who got killed? No, but I heard of her."

"She was my best friend, and it all began with her. I was just starting at Northwestern High, and she was a teacher there. And then Burl, he raped her. But then when he raped her again, she kind of enjoyed it, and so they fell in love. She followed him to Japan and followed him back, and then got killed when her car hit a culvert. And he was so broken up, I tried to do what I could, to ease the sorrow he felt. He'd pick me up after school and buy me a malt, and at night take me out, to the movies or some kind of club. But then I began to feel, it wasn't a torch for her, but more of a lech for me, if I may use such a word."

"Okay, you're telling it like it was."

"So that made me very unhappy, because while I valued him as a friend, and had thought the world of Miss Dale, I didn't like him that way, for a reason I'd rather not tell."

"Nobody's making you do it."

"Next off, comes the invitation. From a girl I knew at school, and after Miss Dale got killed, the best friend I had, I thought. She called, and asked me to spend the night. So she came and picked me up, after Mother said okay, and drove me to her house. This was two months ago. But her mother wasn't there, and I thought it was kind of funny. And then when the boys came, loaded with six-packs of beer, I knew what was up and ducked—or tried to. Because not to mention my morals, which so far had been okay, there was this thing about Burl, which made him repulsive to me.

"So I made a break for the door, but he grabbed me and threw me down. He threw me on the bed, a studio bed that was there in the living room, that my girl friend had fixed up, by pulling the sofa out so it was a bed. Then she and her boyfriend laughed, they laughed real hard at me, and said look at her, look at Little Red Riding Hood, who's going to be et by the wolf, and learn the facts of life. So then they commence guzzling beer."

"Did you guzzle beer?" I asked.

"I don't like it, I can't drink it, no."

"Okay, just asking, that's all."

"Then this girl and her boyfriend did it."

"They——? Did what?"

"Well what do you think?"

"You mean, they just went upstairs and——?"

"No! On the studio bed they did it!"

"Right in front of you?"

"Yes, sir. Right beside me and Burl."

". . . Well! What then?"

"Before I tell about that, I want to explain how it was, when they did it where I could hear. Not where I could see—I couldn't look, I closed my eyes, I had to. But I could hear, and the sounds she made frightened me. I mean they scared me to death! She moaned and wailed and gasped, as though he was torturing her, and I cried and begged him to stop. He didn't and then when they were done, and lying together close, I realized at last that it wasn't pain at all, but joy that was turning her on. And that, for some reason, scared me most of all. But before I could get myself calm, Burl was pawing me. Because he'd been turned on too, exactly the same way she was. And he pawed and pulled at my zipper, trying to get off my dress. And the girl, the one I thought was my friend, said: 'Now, let's give her the works, so she gets it once and for all.' Then they held me, she and her boyfriend, while Burl took off my clothes. And then they opened me up, she holding one of my legs, him the other, and Burl did it to me. It hurt and I bled and I cried, but he didn't stop. Then it was over, and we all lay back, and she said: 'You never regret it, baby—once in a lifetime, but when *that* cherry is gone, life's just a bowl of nice ones.' You understand, Mr. Kirby, I didn't *let* Burl do that. I fought him, I fought the other two, and screamed, or tried to. But her hand was over my mouth, though I bit her. But her only reaction was to laugh at me—as though I was funny."

"So!" I said. "Makes quite a tale, I must say."

"But, Mr. Kirby, there's more."

"Then, let's get it told, by all means."

"When I didn't join in with the laughing, the other boy got scared and blew. He just up and walked out, and she said: 'Oh for God's sake, let him—he's chicken anyway.' Then she commenced wiping me off where I bled, with the towel that she brought. So then Burl decided I'd had enough for one night, and she complimented him on how considerate he was, 'though of course it's tough on you.' And when he asked what she meant by that, she told him, 'If it was me, I'd be looking around for help.' So then he jumped her, and again I heard those terrible sounds that she made, and once more I thought I would die."

". . . You mean Burl had you both?"

"Yes, sir—and she had *them* both."

"All right. And—?"

"They did it one more time, and then at last it was daylight and she took me home. And on the way, she said I shouldn't tell Mother, 'as it's all for your own good, and had to come sooner or later.' I didn't tell, but not for that reason. She's always suspicious of me so I was afraid to. So I said nothing about it. And Burl visited two or three times, wanting to take me out, but I wouldn't go. Then, though, I missed my period, and had a horrible idea why. So I waited and hoped and prayed, but then when no period came I had to go to the doctor and let him give me the test. So when it came back positive he said he had to call Mother. And then holy hell broke loose!

"That was last week, and in all this time I haven't had one kind word or one peaceful moment. She's bad enough, the way she carried on, but he's worse, the goofy ideas he has. They're willing to have the abortion done, but to have an abortion in Maryland, on the basis that I was raped, I have to charge the guy, bring him into court. Because they won't do an abortion just on the girl's say-so to the doctor that unfortunately she was raped, or else they *all* would say that. But Mr. Kirby, I'd rather die—*you* know the stink it would kick up, but they don't as I haven't even told them yet how those other two helped Burl. They insist I have to charge him, and they've given him until sundown to say what he's going to do—you'd think this was a Western.

"And another thing: It's in my father's family to shoot in a case like this. His grandfather killed a guy once, for playing around with his grandmother. It blackened her name, but my father thinks it was wonderful. So now he feels *he* must carry on, except instead of shooting Burl he means to put him in jail."

"Or make him marry you?"

"Oh no. Father knows I wouldn't."

"Then, at sundown, what's he supposed to do?"

"That keeps digging at me. I can't get it out of my head, he's supposed to come up with dough. *That's* what my father's pushing him for."

"He doesn't have any money."

She studied me, then asked, "Are you sure?"

". . . His mother has money, of course—she's not rich, but she's comfortably well-off. However, I can't quite see her kicking in for this."

"And you have dough, Mr. Kirby?"

"Not as much as you might think—I have a business, I make a living. But Burl is twenty-one, and I'm not liable for what he does. So——"

"Mr. Kirby, will you kindly wake up? Come out of that dream you seem to be in? Maybe you're not liable, but you can't turn your back on Burl, and neither can your mother. He's your brother, he's her son, as this whole community knows, and you'll have to stand by him, you and your mother both, whether you want to or not. And then what? You have a business, you say, but will you have one next week, when this stink really gets going? Who wants to do business with a guy who's brother is sitting in jail, for raping a girl in her teens, with the help of two kind friends who are sitting in jail too? I tell you, my father means business, on my behalf, he says, but no matter whose behalf, *you* are under the boom!"

"I've got it, I see it!"

Not that I liked it much, but at least she'd made it clear, where I was at and why, so I could try and figure out what I might do about it. But little by little, as a few minutes went by, I felt things clearing for me—I wouldn't get out of it cheap, but to get out at all was the main thing. She must have sensed I had thought of something, as she leaned forward and waited. "First," I said, "You haven't mentioned yet what you think should be done."

"Well I didn't think I had to. If I don't charge him and I'm not 'titled to the abortion, then I must have the child, which I'm willing to do—I hate it, but I've resigned myself, Mr. Kirby. I'll go to the Crittenton Home, have it, and give it in for adoption—God knows, I won't want to keep it myself. Then I'll take it from there. It won't be easy, and I don't care for the honor of being one of those girls who had to skip a year at school. But——"

"Okay, now we're getting somewhere. Has it occurred to you that what Burl is supposed to say is that he'll pay for the Crittenton Home?"

"Yes, Mr. Kirby, it has."

"Then suppose I offered to pay?"

"Oh, Mr. Kirby, *would* you?"

"Do you know how much it is?"

"Yes sir, all the girls know. Eleven eleven."

"Eleven——?"

"Eleven hundred and eleven dollars. What they do with the odd amount I never found out, buy the baby a rattle, perhaps."

I probably gulped, as it was more than I expected. But I made myself sound cheerful as I yelped: "Fine! Now why don't I call your father, and go over to see him at once."

"Oh, you're sweet!"

She came over and kissed me, a strange, virginal, young girl's kiss that didn't square at all with what we'd been talking about, the condition she was in. I asked for her father's number, and when I called him and said who I was, he was most agreeable, saying: "Oh yes, Mr. Kirby—how are you?" quite as though he knew me, which it turned out later he did. He said he'd look forward to seeing me and gave me the address, which was in University Park, a few blocks away. She was standing by the phone, and her eyes shone when I hung up. I said I was on my way, and that she should stay in the house, "without answering the door or the phone, as I'm known far and wide as a bachelor, and I don't want you to explain." I said I had a luncheon engagement I couldn't break, "but you're my first order of business, and I'll get back as soon as I can, I hope with some really good news."

"All right. I'll stay put until you come."

"Raid the icebox when you get hungry, please."

"It's the best thing I do, eat."

And then, grabbing my arm as I turned to go, and spinning me around: "Mr. Kirby, why don't I say it? We've met before. Don't you remember me?"

"Sonya, I've been having a feeling—"

"At Northwestern High, at Christmastime, when you addressed the school assembly, and said how wonderful it would be if the whole year could be filled with the Christmas spirit. And I fell for you. I really fell for you. And—"

"You played the march? The Wooden Soldiers?"

"And then sat down with you—"

"And asked me to sign your program. And—!"

She laughed, and I knew she knew what I suddenly remembered. Her dress had slipped up, while she was sitting beside me, to show those beautiful legs, the same ones I was looking at now. She kissed me again, this time not so virginal. I got out of there, but fast.

Chapter 3

The Langs lived on Van Buren, in a frame house with shaded trees around it, and I had supposed them strangers to me. But it turned out I knew them both. He was a teller in the Farmers' Trust, and had cashed my checks often, while she worked in a store at the Plaza, and had sold me my upstairs furniture. A plump, middle-aged woman, she let me in, and recalled herself to me. Then she took me into the living room, an airy place with slipcovers on the furniture, where he was waiting. He was a slim, tallish man, with a face not even a mother could be sure of, and one of those quiet, '*Will-you-have-it-in-tens*' voices, like every voice in a bank. However, I placed him at once, and said: "Oh yes, Mr. Lang—we meet again!" She pushed up a chair, he waved me to it, and we all three sat down. And at once a pause ensued, or whatever a pause does—or at least for a long moment, you could hear the clock on the mantelpiece. Then, pretty nervous, I got at it. I said I'd been talking to Sonya, and he said yes, he thought she'd be calling me up. I said I'd come to see if there wasn't some way of "straightening this thing out." He said: "Well that would be up to your brother—actually it was your mother who rang me, asking me to hold off until tonight, but if any straightening is to be done, your brother will have to do it."

Now that news about Mother threw me off, and for a moment I was annoyed that Sonya hadn't mentioned it, but then it occurred to me, perhaps she hadn't known it. Also, his manner, and this news about Burl, that he had to do the straightening if straightening was going to be done, reinforced what I'd smelled, from the way she had acted about it, that something was lurking under cover that I'd had no idea of. So I heard myself tell him, "Well, I'm strictly here on my own. I haven't talked to my brother in a couple of months, or seen my mother since Sunday. If I represent anyone, it's Sonya."

"*I* represent her, Mr. Kirby."

His voice had a bit of a rasp.

"Then, Mr. Lang, suppose we get at it. Do you mind my asking, so I have things perfectly clear, what it was you intended to do, that you held off from at my mother's request?"

"Mr. Kirby, it was you who came to see me."

"Or in other words, get at it?"

"If you don't mind."

My temper was beating a tattoo in my throat, but I swallowed it under control, and told him: "Well, we have two questions, here, as I see it. One is moral, and I don't condone it, or try to minimize it. What my brother did was unspeakable, I dont try to pretend it was not. But I know nothing I can do about it.

"The other question is financial, and about that, there is something I can do, and will, if permitted. As Sonya explained it to me, it comes down to this: If no charges are filed, if the whole matter is dropped, a Maryland abortion is out, and Sonya must have the child. That, she tells me, she's willing to do, and in fact prefers it to what she calls the stink that would surely come if my brother is persecuted. But of course, it will entail a certain expense, especially at the Florence Crittenton Home. *So* in return for your dropping the charges, I'm willing to bear that expense. I can give you a check right now."

Money talks, and I always carry a blank check in my wallet. I slipped it out now, like a magician palming a card, and waved it in front of his eyes. He hardly looked at it. Instead, he asked: "Do you know what the charges will be?"

"Sonya told me, yes."

"And you think the amount you suggest, the Florence Crittenton expense, adequately compensates her?"

"It's compensation for the actual costs."

"It's no compensation at all."

"It's not hay, it's four-figure money."

"But what does it leave *her*? What does *she* get out of it?"

"Well if you put it on that basis—?"

"I do, and you ought to be damned glad! You should be thanking God that I do. Because there's another basis that I could put it on—"

"Louis!" said Mrs. Lang. *"Please!"*

"Our family," he went on, paying no attention to her, "used to farm a place near Waldorf in Charles County, and my grandmother used to sell eggs. She sold eggs that she collected, from women all around, to a storekeeper on the Bryantown Road, who she claimed paid her better than any other. So one Saturday afternoon my grandfather lent her the truck, the little Ford truck that he had, so she could take her eggs in and sell them, and then he walked to Ryon's store, that was across from the railroad station, to see a show that they had.

"And the show was two runt oxen, that an old buzzard drove in every week, to make his week's groceries with. The store kind of helped him out, by keeping silver dollars for him, silver dollars in the till, and how the thing worked was: The old buzzard would find him a sucker, and then bet him a silver dollar that he could throw it down—down in the dirt in front of the store, then roll the cartwheel on it, by word command to the oxen, and then talk them around. He would talk 'em, till they turned the cart clear around, sidewise a step at a time, without coming off the dollar. If they did the dollar was his, his coffee and sugar and flour for the week—but they always did and it was quite a show, that everyone gathered to watch, as he talked to them sweet and low, *'Petty-whoa, petty-whoa, petty-whoa,'* always guiding to the left, and they would work the tongue around, swinging their heads together, braiding and unbraiding their legs. So, Mr. Kirby, on this particular day, the oxen were halfway around, with three-four hundred people gathered around, my grandfather with the rest, when a guy drove up in a Buick, sore as a boil at the storekeeper on the Bryantown Road."

Mrs. Lang stopped up her ears by pushing her fingertips into them, but he kept right on: "'Is that a way to do business?'" he bellowed at everyone. "'On a Saturday afternoon? He's locked up his goddamn store, so he can screw the egg-woman? Couldn't he screw her some other time?'"

"My grandfather borrowed the Buick, ran on out to his place, picked up his thirty-eight, and ran on down to the store, which sure enough was still locked. He called that storekeeper out and shot him through the heart. That's how my family does, when something like this comes up. What wipes out that stain is blood! And short of blood, you ought to be thankful for *anything!* That I don't do to your brother what my grandfather did to that storekeeper! You ought to be down on your knees."

"You said it once, no need to say it twice."

But now Mrs. Lang had taken her fingers out, and told him, very bitter: "You shouldn't have said it! You shouldn't have said it at all! How could you tell him that, with me sitting here, your wife? Why couldn't you have more respect?"

"I tell it all, so he knows what he's up against!"

"You did not! You didn't tell it all! You didn't tell *why* the store was locked up, the real reason, not the one he said, that crazy man in the Buick. It was so he could candle her eggs that the storekeeper locked up his place! She brought in thirteen dozen eggs, and he had to candle them—for that he had to have dark, and that's why he locked up his store! But to keep from getting hung, your grandfather blackened her name, so he could claim the unwritten law! And it broke them up and ruined her life, and I simply do not see how you can brag about it. And I also do not see how you're willing to do what he did, blacken a woman's name, blacken your own Sonya's name, to do in the name of your family what you should be ashamed of."

"I'm not ashamed of it, I'm proud."

"You mean to kill Burl?" I asked him.

"I don't have to say what I mean."

"Oh yes you do, because if you don't, I'm calling the police and filing charges against you. Spit it out! What *do* you mean, Mr. Lang?"

She said: "Louis, you heard him?"

"I mean, on behalf of my child, so she gets compensated, in place of blood to take money."

"I already offered you money."

"Your money, you did. It has to be *his* money. And a great deal more money than the piddling amount you quoted to me."

"He doesn't have any money."

"I happen to know he does have."

"I'm his half brother, I think I know——"

"I work in his bank. I *know* I know."

"Difference of opinion is what makes a horserace."

"Was there something else, Mr. Kirby?"

"I go, I bid you good day."

Mrs. Lang took me to the door, patted my hand, and thanked me for being so considerate of Sonya.

Chapter 4

My mother has one of the few stone houses in this neck of the woods, a pretty little place on Sheridan, a few blocks south of the Langs, and one block north of East-West, an arterial street in Riverdale. I say "little," but actually it's somewhat bigger inside than it looks to be from without. There's a small stone portico, leading to an entrance hall, which is at the side of the house, not in the center, so the living room is quite large, being almost as wide as the house. It has a stone fireplace facing the arch from the hall, and its a bit on the dark side, as the drapes are dark red brocade.

I pulled up around 11:15, parked, and looked for Burl's car. I couldn't see it, but that didn't prove anything, and I admit I was pretty nervous, wondering what I would say if I had to face him. But Mother opened the door, when I was halfway up the walk. She took me in her arms and kissed me, then kissed me again, which for her was the equivalent of a crack-up for somebody else.

She's in her late forties, but looks more like the thirties. She's quite a dish, a bit on the sexy side. She's a bit above medium height, but not what you'd call tall, and though not fat has plenty of shape, especially through the chest. Her hair is dark, with just a streak of gray, her skin pale with an ivory tint. Her face is a little heavy though nicely molded. Her eyes are brown, and not warm, or cold, or anything. They're poker-player's eyes, except that at times, as now, they can be very soft.

"Gramie!" she moaned. "I've been trying to reach you all morning. Oh, thank God you've come!"

Actually, she said "Gawd," in the Virginia way she had, as originally she came from Berryville, being of the Burwell family there, who are proud, perhaps a little too proud, of their relationship to one of Jefferson's secretaries. She was brought to Maryland when young, but sometimes the Old Dominion bleeds through in the way she talks, as when she says *cyard* for *card,* and *gyarden* for *garden,* or *gyowden* as I call it, when I'm having fun with her. But we weren't having fun now, and I just held her close, whispering, "I came the first moment I could, the very first moment I could."

She unwound herself from my arms, took my hand, and led me into the living room, where she sat me down on the sofa, the big one facing the fireplace, and then camped herself down beside me. I went on: "I'd have been here an hour ago, except that I had to see Lang— "

"He's a perfectly horrible man!"

"He's the father of a girl in trouble."

"My heart bleeds for her. Did he let you see her?"

"She came to see me, this morning."

"Oh, then you've *talked* with her?"

I gave it to her quick, what Sonya had told me, at least the highlights of it, then told of my offer to Lang, and the brush he had given it. I asked: "Mother, what does he think he's up to? At my offer, he practically spit in my eye, and then said pointblank he'd take nobody's money but Burl's. But Burl doesn't *have* any money! That stands to reason, and yet Lang says he has, and that he knows he knows. What's it about, do you know?"

"Not really, but I'm terrified."

"Have you given Burl money?"

"Only his allowance, this fifty a week we've kicked in with, you and I together, since he got out of the Army. He could have money, though."

"But *how?* Where would he get it?"

"Gramie, it all goes back to that girl?"

"Little Sonya, you mean?"

"No! The teacher, the one that got killed."

"Oh. I didn't know her."

"A nitwit, but insane about him, about Burl. I think he got sick of her. I think she was messing him up with his—weakness. You know what it is?"

"Women, I would say."

"Yes. Gramie, I haven't plagued you with it, I haven't said anything—partly from not wanting to weep on your shoulder, partly from hating to talk about it, it's so ugly. But you've no idea what it's been like, having him in the house, especially since he got out of the Army. Well, one of the angles has been, I can't keep a servant. Three times it happened, once with a colored girl, twice with white women, and Gramie, the last white woman I got was older than I am. I got her from the agency, and on account of her age thought my problem was solved. He took her while she was fixing dinner—and seemed extra excited by her *because* she was old.

"Gramie, I've tried to inform myself about men of his kind, I've read Casanova's memoirs, and books about Burr, Sickles, and Charles the Second. I don't understand them at all, but this I've found out about them: They're sick, or unbalanced, or something. Strange, offbeat things excite them, as Dale Morgan excited him—till she became a pest. She was a born spinster, pale, colorless, and prissy, but that's what set him off."

"Where does the money come in?"

"I'm coming to that. She was killed when her car hit a culvert wall—her mother was driving, and Burl was here in this room with me, watching a football game. The police didn't even question him. The insurance adjuster did."

"Questioned Burl, you mean?"

"Right here in this room. And at his request—Burl's request—I sat in and answered some questions, too. And a strange thing came out: They'd taken out reciprocal policies, I think that's what they're called, reciprocal accident policies, his in her favor, hers in his—five thousand for loss of a limb, twenty-five thousand for loss of life, and double indemnity for death in a motor accident. Burl kept telling the adjuster: 'It was all her idea—I thought it was screwy myself. But she was paying for it, and who was I to object?' Gramie, that money had to be paid, the whole fifty thousand, and I'm all but certain it has been."

"Then Lang was right?"

"He should know what Burl's balance is."

"Then let Burl pay, why not?"

She tightened, then went on: "One night, not long after that, a boy showed up here, whose name I don't recall, but Burl called him Al. He'd been in the Army with Burl, in Japan, in the headquarters motor pool, keeping trucks, cars, and motorcycles in running order. And he got slopped on beer and talked—mainly about girls, in tea houses, shops, and bars, which I thought an odd subject in front of me, but I indulge all former soldiers. But then suddenly he remembered Bong, and I thought Burl was trying to shush him, by changing the subject, by being reminded of other things. But Al kept right on. I judge Bong's name was Bin Ben Bon, but Al called him Bing Bang Bong, and revelled in his exploits. Bong was a South Vietnamese, who had done undercover work, and special sabotage in Hanoi. And he would boast of how he had killed

Hanoi generals, four of them, he said, four 'genetor,' it seemed he called them, by loosening a certain screw, a set-screw in the steering assembly, of these North Vietnamese generals' cars. 'One slet-sclew,' he boasted to Al and Burl. 'Come here rook I show you, one 'slet-screw' in generor car, a generor clash, generor die in ditch.' Al thought him killingly funny, but I didn't. I had a horrible suspicion I'd heard the truth at last about poor little Dale Morgan's death."

". . . Be a pretty hard truth to prove."

"Gramie, does Lang have to prove it?"

"Go on, say what you're leading to."

"What I'm leading to is: I think Lang wants that money, a big hunk of what Burl was paid – *if* he was paid, as I imagine he was – but I don't think that's all he wants. I think he wants to ruin Burl, as a matter of sheer vindictiveness – break the thing wide open before consenting to be bought off – but not before reopening that other case. Because if the police find out that he was paid that money, they'll have to reopen that case."

"But they must know it already."

"Right, and then this will force their hand."

Now, for the first time, I went into details, on the rape I mean, telling stuff I'd left out before, especially that other couple, but she wouldn't let me finish. "Please! I can't listen to it," she said, "I can't bear any more! Oh, what a filthy, rotten thing!"

"Incidently, why the sundown bit?"

". . . On that, I think I did right."

"Yeah, but what was the idea of it?"

"To give Burl time to skip."

"Oh. Oh, I see. Well – did he?"

"Not till I kicked in with money. Can you imagine that? That tremendous sum he was paid, and still he sandbagged me for five hundred dollars. It's why I couldn't call you sooner. I had to go to the bank for cash."

I got out my blank check, the same one I had waved at Lang, and got ready to kick in with my share. But actually

I wrote five hundred, the whole bite. When she saw that figure, though, she lifted my hand, the one with the pen in it, and kissed it. "Gramie," she said, "I love it when you give me money—it makes my heart go bump, that's the woman of it. But this I can't take off you. No—it's on me for being so dumb. For having him here at all. For——"

Suddenly she stiffened, broke off, and then asked me: "Gramie, you talked to this girl—where? Where is she now?"

"At my house. I thought I said."

"Then, until we know where we're at, keep her there! Don't let her go home! Because this is what terrifies me: Dale Morgan is dead—that we know. But it would simplify Burl's problem, put him in the clear, if this girl were to die, too—accidentally, of course, as Dale Morgan died. It mustn't happen."

"Listen, I can't lock her up."

"You'll have to do *something,* Gramie."

She stared at me, then went on: "Perhaps Burl has skipped, perhaps not. Perhaps he's out there somewhere, just biding his time. And if he knows where she is——!"

It was hard for me to believe, to get through my head at all, that she was talking in earnest. I mumbled I'd try to think of something, and then she asked me: "Would you like me to ring Jane Sibert? And call off your luncheon engagement?"

"I can't. I drew some cash too, her allowance for the next four weeks, that I thought I'd hand her before she leaves, as kind of a going-away surprise——"

"Then, you must go. She's important to us."

"What time is it?"

"Twelve-ten. You'd better be running along."

I kissed her, told her: "I'll be in touch, I'll keep you posted. After Jane goes I have to see Sonya, and report to her how

I came out. Perhaps she'll have some idea on how to keep under cover."

"Is she nice? Or what?"

"She's damned easy to look at."

Chapter 5

So why was Jane Sibert important, and why did I have to go? Well, she was a widow who lived on a little farm, a place of sixty-seven acres, in back of College Park, and I've already told how she took me in, when I was fifteen years old, becoming a sort of foster mother to me, so I wouldn't have to live with my stepfather. It was a wonderful place for a boy, and I loved it for ten or twelve years, but it was not such a wonderful place for a middle-aged woman, trying to live there alone—after I pulled out, I mean. And yet she was *sot,* as she called it, and instead of selling her farm, persisted in living on it, as she had in the days of her marriage, when the University of Maryland, whose campus abutted her fields, was the Maryland Agriculture College, and things were simple and friendly and small. So of course the catch was her assessment. Once it was upped to bring it in line with adjoining properties, which were so valuable it took your breath, she'd be eaten alive by taxes. To head that off, to retain her "rural agriculture" status, the place had to *be* agricultural, meaning she had to farm it.

Not herself knowing a rake from a buzz saw, she found a guy out near Berwyn, who had all the required machinery and was willing to go shares with her, making a crop of hay. Then alfalfa it was, but when all deductions were made, it didn't bring in much cash. So to kind of equalize, so she could go on living in style, I made her a little allowance—not so little actually, as one hundred dollars a week is a drain on anyone's income, and I can't say I didn't feel it.

Understand: There'd been an arrangement before, with my mother kicking in for my board on the farm, my expenses at Yale, and the money I needed to start out in the real estate business. But once I was on my own, her contribution stopped, and mine began. That is, I became Jane's paying boarder, bearing part of the farm's expenses. But when I moved to my house, I had it out with Jane, as to what it would do to her finances. The answer was: She could manage. But that "manage" sounded pinched, and considering everything, how I felt about her, what she'd done for me, and how pretty she was, I said she wouldn't have to "manage," as I'd keep my payments up. Then she surprised me and shook me down to my heels. In a quiet little speech, she said she'd been waiting for that, actually hoping for it, to know if I'd be so kind, without any hint from her. So, she went on, since I did come through so "gallantly," she would make me her sole beneficiary, in the new will she was having drawn, she having no close relatives she had to consider. Or in other words, I would come into her land.

Or in still other words, I could have my own development, sure to make me at least a million dollars. But it would mean more than that hunk of money, tremendous though it was. It would mean the realization of a dream, the one Mother mentioned, that I'd been having for years, in regard to Southern Maryland, of which Prince Georges County is part. It's east and south of the District of Columbia, not on the northern side, where Montgomery County lies and Western Maryland begins—and the winter winds blow. I meant to start a development that would hook weather into the promotion, that would smash up the advantage Montgomery County has had, in appealing to moneyed people, and offer property on the basis that Prince Georges is Dixie, which it is. I'd lived in Montgomery, at Cabin John on the Potomac, and seen all those blizzards go whistling down the river, which is beautiful in winter, with the rocks all covered with ice, and so cold even a brass monkey couldn't take it.

"Southern Maryland *is* Dixie," I told the Rotarians one day. "Let us never forget what Lucky Baldwin told them, out in California, when they complained he was charging too much for the land around Santa Anita. 'The land?' he roared at them, 'hell, we give the land away. We're selling *climate*.'"

I've been hipped on the subject, and this farm, if I ever came into it, would give me the chance to make the hook-up of climate with the promotion, and take the play away from Montgomery, so Prince Georges would be *the* place, instead.

So that's why I kept pinching myself, after I left her that day, to make sure it wasn't a dream I'd wake up from. Of course, I couldn't make any move to check on any stuff, like water, sewers, and power, as it would have been a little like imagining how pretty she'd look in her coffin. But Mother could do it for me, in a quiet way under cover, through political connections she has—and also, she jumped at the chance of coming in with me, of being my financial backer, and she got on the ball quick. Inside of a month, she reported everything clear. All lights were green whenever the cards said go.

So that's why Jane was important, in a business way, and personally. I was to pick her up at home, at the old farmhouse, with its 1910 front porch, that I itched to rip off, substitute a modern entrance, add garage and rec room as wings, and in that way make a Southern mansion out of it. It had a circular drive out front, a mudhole in winter and dustbowl in summer, and it didn't make me feel better right now, that when I turned into it a Caddy was parked out front, which meant of course that these people she was leaving with, for a month's tour of Canada, had already come for her, and that I'd have to ask them to lunch.

When she opened the door I did it big, taking her in my arms, smacking her full of kisses, and patting her on the bottom. She's a pert little thing in her sixties, with a trim figure, pink face, and white hair that she rinses blue. She was in some kind of cotton suit, and held me close for more kisses, out there in the front porch.

Then she introduced me to her friends, who stepped outside with us, a couple by the name of Hamell, and I give you one guess how much interest I took in them. But with the old Maryland spirit, I pumped their hands, asked them to lunch and wouldn't take no for an answer. So then we started out, the ladies with me in my car, he following along in his. The idea was that after lunch they'd come back and pick up the bags, then drive to Philadelphia, where they'd pick up another lady, and then head north and tour Canada for a month. "Fine, fine, fine," I said, though what was fine about it I didn't know then and don't know now.

I took them to the Royal Arms, which served us a nice lunch. We talked mainly of Canada, and I kept cautioning Hamell to take it easy on the Canadian roads. "They're okay," I said, "well-built and well-graded, but they have an item called frost, so they bulge and buckle and break."

"There's no frost in Prince Georges," said Jane.

"There is, but not much."

"Prince Georges County is Dixie."

At last, this endless lunch was over and we went out on the big portico that overlooks the parking lot, where Jane lingered with me while the Hamells went down for their car. I took the envelope I'd sealed up the night before out of my pocket, and handed it over to her. It contained four weeks' allowance, four hundred dollars in twenties, and I said: "I thought it might come in handy, while you're traveling around."

She opened it, counted it, and looked at the gag card I'd put in. Then she pulled my face down and kissed me. "You look like Handsome Dan," she said. Handsome Dan was the original Yale bulldog, whose picture she'd seen on one of her trips to New Haven, visiting me. Then she kissed me again, and said: "Your kept woman thanks you."

"Why do you say things like that?" I asked her. "I'm under a thousand obligations to you, and if now and then I try to return the favor, I'm only too glad. You needn't take cracks at yourself."

"Cracks? I thought I was bragging."

She looked at me somewhat peculiarly, then asked: "Have you seen your mother lately?"

"I was with her this morning, yes."

"She's in a spot."

"*She's* in a spot? What about *me?*"

Now if mentally we'd really been in tune, that was her cue to say something, to get in there with it, to give me something to chew on. But, close though we were, in a way, on that level we never seemed to make it. She gave it the back of her hand, in spite of my upset, which I didn't try to conceal. "Oh I wouldn't worry about it," she trilled in a very bland way. "It's depressing, and must be damned annoying. Just the same it could be worse. Not saying that Burl should not be ashamed of himself. He's a handsome boy, but wayward, very wayward."

"What he did to that girl was inexcusable."

"Oh, don't waste any tears on her—one perhaps, but not a bucketful. She'll get over it. She's not the first girl, and won't be the last, to get caught under the gate. Frailty, thy name is woman, don't forget."

"Unfortunately, this was a slight case of rape."

"Oh it always is when Mommy finds out." Then, as though none of it amounted to much: "If I were you, though, and you can afford it, I'd pick up the tab—it might relieve the tension. I mean the Florence Crittenton charges."

"I thought of that. I made the offer."

". . . And?"

"Declined—with a kick in the teeth."

"Keep trying, Gramie."

The car rolled up, I took her down and put her in, and that was all that we said on the subject. I'd have given anything for something helpful out of her, and she didn't seem to know it. I kissed her good-bye, shook hands with the Hamells, stood back and watched them roll off. Then I found my own car and started once more for my own headache.

Chapter 6

I had told her not to answer the bell, so I let myself in with my key, and didn't see anything of her, but caught the smell of furniture polish. I went in the living room and she wasn't there, but the smell was, even stronger than in the hall, and I was surprised at how slick everything looked, especially the bookshelves, which are maple, and showed the grain of the wood in a way I'd never noticed before. I was opening my mouth to call, when she whirled past the arch that led to the hall, a dust mop in her hand, which she shook out the front door, first taking a peep out to make sure no one was looking.

But her costume was really quite startling. It consisted of one of my shirts, with the sleeves buttoned back on her elbows—and that was all, at least that I could see, except for her shoes and a tea cloth bound on her head. Her legs were bare, but there popped in my mind an impression, which I'd got from peeping before, that she hadn't had garters on, which of course meant panty hose. But if she'd taken them off, what did she have on now? I was working on it, as she started back to the kitchen, when all of a sudden she saw me and gave a yelp.

"Oh!" she said. "Oh!"

"Yeah," I answered. "Hello."

"What did he say? No wait, I'll clean myself up."

She started for the kitchen again, but stopped again and popped out: "Well *you* said 'cleaning woman,' but I wouldn't go that far. This was the *dirtiest* place! And I thought I could clean it for you. You've been so nice to me, it was the least I could do, to show my 'preciation."

"You're quite wonderful, Sonya."

"Well? Does it look nice?"

"So shined up I hardly know it."

"Be back."

She went scampering back to the kitchen, and I heard the water running. Then she was there again, saying: "Innyhow, my hands are clean. So? What did he say?"

"He said no. I doubled the ante, as a matter of fact, upped it to twenty-two twenty-two—and he still said no. I went to bat and struck out."

"I was kind of hoping he'd take it."

"So was I—I was stunned at his reaction."

Then, being careful of what I said, especially to keep Mother out of it, her trick to let Burl skip, and her suspicions of how the teacher got killed, with the possible money angle, I gave a few more details of what her father had said, telling her: "As well as I can make out, he means to wreak a revenge, on Burl, as a matter of family honor, and then get money for you, as the price for reversing his gears. But it has to be Burl's money, and I may as well tell you that things came out in our talk, to arouse suspicions in me, that you may not know about——"

"You mean, in connection with Dale Morgan?"

"Then you *do* know about them?"

"I don't know about *innything*. But my father kept plaguing me, after Dale Morgan died, about the insurance she may have carried"—she called it *shurance*—"in Burl's favor. But I know nothing to tell him—is that what you're talking about?"

"As I pieced things together, yes."

"Family honor's bugging him."

". . . I can't picture him using a gun."

"He wouldn't have the nerve. But he has to do *something,* something for *me* he thinks, and has decided to settle for money. But to prove he means business, Mr. Kirby, I think he means to charge Burl. That's what scares me so, that he'll swear out a warrant for him."

"That's about as I figure it out."

"And that will bring the newspapers in."

She sat there in her old place on the sofa, I in my old placc across from her, and for some time nothing was said, though she kept staring at me. Then I remembered Mother's warning. "By the way," I said. "You shouldn't go home tonight. You shouldn't be anywhere Burl is likely to find you."

"You mean he might try to kill me?"

". . . Well—not exactly that."

"Then, exactly what?"

"Okay—that. He raped you, didn't he?"

"And killed Dale Morgan, Mr. Kirby."

"Sonya! He couldn't have! He wasn't there!"

"And her mother was driving. He killed her, though."

"But how? How?"

"I don't know how, Mr. Kirby."

She leaned forward, both hands on her knees, looked me straight in the eye, and went on: "I tell you one thing, though: My father knows how, and we'd better do something quick, or he'll blow this ship out of water. And that could ruin us both. Both, do you hear, Mr. Kirby? I said——"

"I heard what you said, Sonya."

We sat blinking at each other, and then in a low voice she said: "There's one way out, Mr. Kirby, that'll settle Burl's hash, settle my father's hash, and settle *my* hash, for that matter—I mean, from *your* point of view. One way out for you, that would be a whole lot cheaper than the Crittenton charges would be. One way out that would take care of everything."

"What way is that, Sonya?"

"You could marry me yourself."

". . . I bet I could, *I bet I could!*"

If she'd set off a cherry bomb under me, she couldn't have jolted me worse, and I didn't try to hide it, how her idea hit me. She didn't move or raise her voice, merely telling me: "Well don't fly off the handle. I mean it."

"Sonya, I think you're feeling the strain."

"I am, I admit it, and you better."

"Let's stick to what makes sense."

"This does, if you'll let me explain it."

"I'm sorry, I couldn't keep a straight face."

"Then I'll explain it innyway, and if your face gets all twisted up, from how funny it is to you, then okay it's funny to you, but it's not funny to me, so suppose you hold still and listen and stop making silly cracks."

"You talk like a wife already."

"You ready?"

"Then, make with the explanation."

"You go to Northwestern High, you hear things all the time, because some girl's always in trouble, and the rest of them talk about it, coming up with stuff that doesn't come up in sex-education class. So you and I get married, and that makes you my guardian—not my father inny longer, or my mother, or innyone, but you. So that gives you the right to have an abortion done, in *New York,* where all they want is your money, two hundred dollars, please pay the cashier. So, two hundred, plus the plane fare, plus the hotel bill, is a whole lot cheaper isn't it, than the Florence Crittenton Home? It would wind the whole thing up, because you'll be the one, remember, who decides if Burl's to be charged, if a warrant's going to be sworn out. If you say no, that's it. So? Does that make sense or doesn't it?"

". . . Okay. And then what?"

"What do you mean? And then what?"

"We come back from New York and then what?"

"Well that would be up to you."

"Hey! This was your idea. What's the rest of it?"

"The rest of it is, it would be up to you, to keep me or ship me home, and whichever way you want, I won't be inny pest. Of course, I'd feel I owed you something, nice as you've been to me, and maybe you wouldn't mind. But, if you didn't feel that way, you could get a divorce, or 'nullment I think its called, on account of me not being consummated. Of course, I own up, I would try being nice to you, so nice you might want to keep me, without shipping me back. At least, you don't think me repulsive."

"How do you know what I think?"

"By how you look at my legs."

"Well who wouldn't, the way you throw them around?"

"Now you talk like a husband."

"Well, it makes more sense than I realized, and I confess the guardian angle hadn't occurred to me. *But*—"

"It would fix everything up—Burl, Father, Mother, honor, the whole stinking mess. We could apply for a license today, pick it up, be married Monday, go to New York Monday night, and have the surgery done on Tuesday—it takes a minute and a half. And then Tuesday night with me in your lap, helping you make up your mind, you could say what you want to do."

"The answer has to be no."

"Want to bet?"

". . . Bet? Bet what?"

"What do you think? Money."

She fished under one heel and came up with a dime she put on the table. "I always keep it in my shoe," she said, "for luck – but sometimes it comes in handy. You covering it?"

I put down a dime, saying, "Taking candy from a child."

"Okay, twenty cents in the pot."

With that she unbuttoned the shirt, took it off, and draped it on the sofa. She was naked as when she was born. "Goddam it," I snapped. "*put that shirt back on!*"

"Goddam it, I won't."

She walked a few steps toward the hall, switching her bottom at me. Then she stopped and began turning around. "I model myself for you," she explained, "so you see what the rest of me looks like. So you see what you're getting."

As she turned she talked: "Leftside – backside. Is it pretty?"

"You know damned well it is."

"Yeah, but I like to be told. Right side — "

"Very nice."

"Front?"

"That'll do! I'm not looking."

"Oh yes you are, you're peeping!"

"If so, it was a slip."

"We all can yield to temptation."

"Sonya, you're beautiful, I'm so excited I can't talk, and yet – we're barely acquainted — "

"I'm not done yet, I've barely started."

She gave a hop, skip, and jump, and landed beside me on the sofa. I stiffened, so as not to fold her in, or respond if she tried to kiss me. But kissing me wasn't the idea. She started unbuttoning my shirt, first pulling my necktie aside, until it was open down to my belt, and then pushing her face inside, and nuzzling into my armpit. Then she began to inhale, but slowly, as though concentrating. After some moments of that she seemed to wilt, crumpled in my arms, and lay with her eyes closed, her head against my chest. I wouldn't have been human if I didn't hold her close, or notice how soft she was, and warm, and how silky her skin. Pretty soon she opened her eyes, and began whispering to me, "Okay, Mr. Kirby, I'll say it, why I could like Burl Stuart, across the drugstore table, and couldn't *stand* him that other way, or possibly marry him. Mr. Kirby, he stinks. Maybe he's your brother, maybe he smells nice to others, but to me he smells like feet. He makes me sick to my stomach. But you don't, you have a heavenly smell!" I said I smelled like Russian Leather, the face lotion I use, but she said: "It's not that, it's you. You smell like grass, grass that's just been cut. I noticed it that first day, when I sat down bcsidc you in school—maybe that's why my dress slipped up, and you first peeped at my legs. And then you caught me again today, sniffing you in the car. I had to know if you still smelled the same way—and you did. And do. It's why I took that shirt out of the laundry basket, instead of finding a clean one. I knew it would smell like you. How do *I* smell, to *you?*"

She lifted a swatch of her hair and dusted it over my nose. "Beautiful," I whispered. "Just beautiful."

"Hold me close."

"I am holding you close."

"Pat me."

I patted her on the bottom, both sides.

"Paddywhack me."

"I couldn't make myself."

"Mr. Kirby, I could give myself to you, *now.*"

"Sonya, it must not, it *cannot* be!"

"I said *could*—not that I'm going to. I can't, I know it, not with this thing inside—it would be messy, it wouldn't be decent. Till Tuesday we have to hold off. My that's a long time, Saturday, Sunday, Monday, Tuesday—I'm going to suffer. Are you?"

"Yes, it's going to be hell."

"But then, Tuesday night, I promise you—"

"Shut up, stop tempting me!"

"Can I pick up the money?"

". . . You win. Pick it up."

Chapter 7

She gave me a long, hot kiss and I thought about God. Then she looked at my watch and jumped up. "It's going on for three," she whispered, "I have to get dressed." She grabbed the shirt and scampered upstairs, I following after, for what reason I have no idea, unless for the ancient intimacy of watching a woman dress. Her clothes were on my bed, such few clothes as she had, and she got them on pretty quick, first taking off her shoes and putting a dime in each heel. "Now I have two dimes," she said. "Should bring me all kinds of luck." She got into her panty hose, then into her shoes, and then picked up her dress.

"Hold it!" I interrupted. Aren't you forgetting something? Like, for instance, your bra? Where is it, by the way?"

But that drew a blank stare. "I don't wear inny bra," she informed me. "I don't need inny bra—here, I'll show you."

She caught hold of my hand and guided it, so it covered one of this beautiful protuberances, and I felt a touch of vertigo, from how warm it was, how soft, and how firm. "Well?" she asked. "Does that need a bra."

"No," I gasped. "Come on, hurry up."

She pulled the dress over her head, zipped it, and put on her hat, after combing her hair at the mirror. "Okay," she said. "Now we better call home. They'll have to come with us, you know, Mother and Father both, so they can sign the consent, parental consent, it's called. On account of me being so young."

"Yes," I said. "you'd better call."

She sat on the bed, picked up the phone on the night table and punched the buttons. But then I took the receiver. "Better I talk," I said.

It was Mr. Lang who answered. I said who I was and went on: "Sir, I think now we're all straightened out on this little problem of ours. I neglected to tell you before, but Sonya and I are old friends—we met at a school assembly, at Northwestern High, when she played the march at assembly, and I made the Christmas address. We got along famously then, and talking it over today, in a thorough frank way, we've decided we are going to be married—which of course will pretty well take care of everything. But, on account of her age, we must have your consent, yours and Mrs. Lang's, which is what I'm calling about."

I stopped on purpose,expecting him to come in and say what he had to say. But I waited and no answer came. I asked, "Mr. Lang, are you there?"

"Yeah, I'm here," he said.

"Well? What do you say?"

"What is there *to* say, Mr. Kirby?"

That didn't quite seem to cover it, and I pressed him, as to whether he'd sign the consent, and whether Mrs. Lang would. But no answer came, and then I could hear her voice, but couldn't hear what she said. Then came that blank you get when somebody cups the phone. Then the blank went off and her voice came through: "Mr. Kirby, my husband just told me what you and Sonya are fixing to do, and I can only say: God bless! Mr. Kirby, I've always admired you so, and want you to know how grateful I am, how grateful we both are, that you'd step into the breach this way, and—"

"But I want to step into the breach!"

"And it's so decent of you, Mr. Kirby—"

"Mrs. Lang, about the parental consent—"

"And Mr. Kirby, one other thing—"

But on that, Sonya grabbed the receiver. She'd been cuddled into my arms, so she could hear, and she let her mother have it: "Mother! This is me! Now will you knock it off with the goo, all this ladylike talk? It's getting late, and we have to apply for our license—we want to do it today, so we can be married Monday and get it over with! But we must have your consent, and—" But there was more talk from the other end, and suddenly Sonya screamed, "Yah! Yah! Yah"—or something that sounded like that, and began jawing stuff that seemed wild, but that apparently did the trick. Then she snapped: "Okay, we'll be by in ten minutes! See that you don't keep us waiting! We have to be there before that bureau, the Marriage License Bureau, closes down for the day! Ten minutes!"

She put the receiver back, stood up, smoothed her dress, and kissed me. "Okay, let's go," she said. "We're set."

So started an afternoon and evening that melted into a blur, that was something like a dream, and yet at the same time was real. They were waiting out front, Mrs. Lang in a black silk dress with red flowers on it, he in a suit, with no hat. I hopped out, kissed her, and shook hands with him. I handed her in, let him climb in beside her, closed them up, got in myself, and started out. He said, "Mr. Kirby, I don't try to read your mind, but if it was me, I'd want it done kind of quiet, so how about Rockville instead of

Marlboro? I imagine you're not so well-known in Montgomery County, as you are here in Prince Georges, and—"

"Good!" I answered. "Sonya?"

"Well of course," she chirped. "It's how we should do, of course. It's amazing, dumb as he is, the things my father thinks up."

"He's due to get brighter. Did you know?"

"He *is?* So he won't be so dumb inny more?"

"It's a well-known fact—when smart-alecky kids get older, their parents get un-dumbed."

"Well what do you know. But, take the dumbness out—"

"Sonya," I said. "Shut up."

"Okay."

She said it meek, opened her legs, and began fanning herself with her skirt. "Mother," she asked, "if you had told me that, what then?"

"You'd have screamed for an hour, at least."

"He tells me shut up and I shut."

"And a great improvement, I'd say."

That was Mr. Lang, and it hit us all funny, so we laughed and eased off a bit. For the rest of the trip to Rockville we acted natural and chatted along, mainly about what a fine day it was. When we got there, I parked in front of the courthouse and we all went in, marching up to the Marriage License Bureau, where the lady was quite friendly, and it turned out they had printed forms for the parental consent. So while the Langs were filling that out, Sonya and I filled out our application and signed it. Then the lady looked everything over and said: "This seems to be in order—you can pick up your license Monday." I asked if "the judge" could marry us, that being a brevet I'd heard of, that seemed suitable to a courthouse bigwig. But from the smile she gave it I knew I'd pulled a blooper.

"Actually," she said, "it's against the law in Maryland for a judge to perform a marriage, but the deputy clerk would be glad to. Do you wish to make an appointment?"

"Well I certainly *hope* so!" said Sonya, in such a hard-boiled way that the lady laughed and we all laughed.

But Mrs. Lang started to cry. "*There* now!" said the lady. "*There* now! *There!*"

We set it for two o'clock, which would give us time in the morning for things that might have to be done.

Going back it was still very friendly, but with long pauses between, and no laughing, or at least, not much. I expected opposition, perhaps quite a fight, over my taking Sonya for the weekend, and was rehearsing argument for it, for some little time in my mind, before bringing the subject up. But when I did, there was no opposition. "I may as well own up," said Mr. Lang, "I used bad judgment about it, about this idea I had, that though blood is what wipes out that stain, money can take its place. It was for her benefit, Sonya's I mean, that I must say for myself, so at least my intentions were good. What I hadn't realized was, I was creating a situation where one person on earth could wish Sonya dead, could benefit from having her dead, on account of a situation I'd created myself. And not to go into details, I can't honestly say that person would stop at killing her. So, until Monday, when this marriage takes place and this person no longer has reason to take her life we're up against something quite serious. That's why, Mr. Kirby, I'll let Sonya go with you—otherwise, I'd blister her backside for doing it."

"No blistering's called for, I promise you."

"Your intentions do you credit."

"Mr. Kirby, we trust you completely," said Mrs. Lang, and a silence settled down. Then presently he asked me: "You taking her to New York?"

"... That idea had occurred to us."

"To *me!*" yelped Sonya. "*I* thought it up."

"It occurred to *me,* Mr. Kirby."

"Well listen to him! Maybe he's *not* so dumb!"

She twisted around to stare at her father, and I said: "I told you, didn't I? That he was due to get brighter?"

"It's amazing, simply amazing."

"But I was too set in my mind," he went on, paying no attention to her, "thinking about that money, that I wouldn't let myself face it, that this simple solution was there."

"It *was* Sonya's idea, that's true."

"So let's all bow down and give thanks."

She was quite airy about it, but her father gave it a brush. "I give thanks to Mr. Kirby," he announced, in an extra-solemn way, "for relieving a situation in all kinds of different ways, especially for me. At least, I'm off the hook."

I didn't say anything, but it seemed to me he accented *I'm* just a little. And Sonya caught it too. "*You're* off the hook?" she snapped. "What's that supposed to mean? That somebody else in on?"

"It means what I said. I'm off."

"It sounded to mean more."

"Don't hear sounds that weren't made."

They may have wrangled a little more, but I didn't pay too much attention, as we were nearing the Lang home, and I had to take up the question of where I would go with her, these next three days and three nights, as taking her home was out of the question. I mean, if she were coming in as my wife next week, then to have her lay up for the weekend as an unexplained what-is-it? would be giving her unnecessary problems. And so the subject of who was on the hook got dropped—but it didn't stay dropped, I assure you. It kept coming up and coming up and coming up.

Chapter 8

The Langs asked me in, and I waited with them in the living room while Sonya went upstairs to pack an overnight bag. I said what was on my mind, and favored Washington, D.C., for our hideout, as being near if something came up, and at the same time completely safe. I mentioned the Mayflower Hotel, "which is much like home to me, as I've been there so often." The Mayflower got instant approval. Then Sonya came down, carrying her bag, and I broke the news to her, telling her, "I'll sign you in as my fiancée, taking a single and a bath for you. For myself I'll take a suite, and that way, without violating any rules, you can visit me any time, and we won't have to meet in the lobby."

She said, "We're going to Ocean City, and you're signing me in 'and wife,' in a suite with bath for two." I hit the roof, saying: "Do you want to get me arrested? How can I possibly get away with it, coming in with a child and signing her on as my wife—unless, except, and until I have the papers to prove it, which I won't have until Monday." Her father and mother agreed, but she paid not the slightest attention, standing in front of a wall mirror, working on her face. Then she took off her hat, opened her bag, took something out and pulled it on her head, putting the hat back on. Then she turned around, a grown woman.

She sashayed over to me, a bit heavy in the bottom, and told me: "What gives a young girl away, a young girl trying to look older, is her walk—the way she skips around like a heifer. A woman has lead in her tail."

"Well thank you, Sonya," snapped Mrs. Lang.

"Don't be ashamed of it, Mother—it makes the world go 'round. But if you're a young girl and want to look older——"

"What's that on your head?" I asked her.

"The wig I wore when I played Mrs. Malaprop at the school entertainment. It has streaks of gray in it."

"And what have you done to your face?"

"Made it up, using the liner. You put on one thin, vertical line, over the nose in the middle, and two slanting lines alongside the mouth, leading down toward the jaw. That's all—with those three lines you can pass, so no one will ever guess. One thing you *can't* change, or do *innything* about, is your voice, that Mia Farrow mumble a young girl always has. So what you do about *that* is keep your mouth shut."

"You think you can?" asked her father.

"I'll do my best. No one can do inny more."

"Then suppose you start practicing *now.*"

We all laughed some more, but I noticed that now she looked so much older, no argument was made by anyone against signing her in "and wife." I said, "At Ocean City, I've heard that the Pocahontas is one of the best motels, and if I may borrow the phone, I'll reserve our space right now."

The phone was in the hall, and I put a $5 bill under it, but Mrs. Lang picked it up and slipped it in my breast pocket, saying: "*Please,* Mr. Kirby, *please!*"

The Pocohontas did have space, "what we call our efficiency suite," the reservation clerk said, "—sitting room, bedroom, bath, and kitchenette, with pulldown beds in the sitting room. All in all, if you're bringing the family, there's accommodations for six."

"It's just myself and my wife," I told him.

"Then I'm sure you'll find it satisfactory."

"How much is it setting me back?"

"Thirty-eight a day, two-fifty by the week."

"We'll be there until Monday morning."

"And when shall we expect you, sir?"

"Tonight, some time after ten."

He took my name and number, in case something came up, and when I hung up Sonya said: "I just loved it, how he said 'and my wife.' It's what I want to be, his wife."

"You get along quite well," said Mrs. Lang.

"I'm stuck on him, that's why. More'n he is on me."

"You got a stuckometer, to measure?" I asked her.

"Maybe not, but I know. I'm working on it, though."

I called Miss Musick, to say I wouldn't be in until Tuesday. I said: "Something's come up, kind of a continuation of that call, the one you took from the girl. Miss Musick, I'm getting married."

"Oh! Oh! Oh!"

"To her, the one you talked to."

"But Mr. Kirby, do I know her?"

"I don't think so, but she wants to know you."

"I knew there was something about her!"

"You can say that again, Helen."

Then at last we were headed for Ocean City, but I still had nothing to sleep in, and thought it most inadvisable to stop by the house and pack, as popping in with a young girl, and then popping out with her and a packed bag would be almost as bad as having her there for the weekend. But she knew what to do. "People's," she said, "will have everything you need—you name it, they'll tell you which counter it's on." So we stopped by People's in College Park, and sure enough they fixed me up, not only with pajamas, shirts, razor, lather, lotion, comb, and brush, but also luggage, a snappy zipper bag, exactly what I should have to stop at a beach motel. While I was buying my stuff, I gave her twenty dollars, to buy whatever she needed, but she didn't buy anything. "I'm being economical," she said, "to prove I'm a sensible wife." But I'd bought something for her, a nice big bottle of Arpege, which she held close and almost cried over. "I never had any scent!" she kept saying over and over. "No scent of my own at all—I always had to steal Mother's. And this is the kind I love!"

So, when at last we really got rolling, it was a happy time. She kept sniffing the Arpege bottle, opening her legs, and fanning herself with her skirt. Then she took off the wig, put it in her bag, and wiped away the lines. "They can wait," she said. "Just right now I want to be *me*."

We crossed the bay on the bridge, I would say around seven o'clock, and then ran for some distance by daylight, through the flat Eastern Shore country. Then we spotted a place called The Grisfield, which looked to be fairly decent, and decided to stop for dinner. It was the first I found out how much she could eat. Their specialty was crab, which I don't really care for too much, so after she spoke for it, I ordered the Delmonico steak. "Well," she said kind of sheepish, "can I have what I want? Can I have what I *really* want?" I said of course, and she said: "I want the crab *and* the steak!" The waitress let out a whistle, and said: "Your daughter's really hungry."

"I'm his wife!" snapped Sonya, pretty sore.

That upset the girl, and she said: "I'm sorry!"

However, I played it straight. "One steak dinner for me," I said. "One steak dinner *and* one crab dinner for my wife."

"Yes sir."

"The nerve of that twerp," said Sonya, after the girl had gone, "calling me your daughter. How did *she* know who I was?"

"Brat," I said, "easy does it. She was merely trying to be friendly. Wipe your nose—and shut up."

"Okay."

She ate fruit cup, two crab cakes with tartar sauce, cole slaw, steak, baked potato, string beans, and apple pie à la mode, while the waitress stood off and gaped. I asked: "Do you know what you look like?"

"Cow, chawing her cud."

"I was going to say a Raphael cherub—cute."

"Tell it like it is. I love to eat."

"I love to see you."

"It's going to cost you something, feeding me."

A pay phone was up near the door and I had the waitress bring me two dollars in quarters, telling Sonya, "I'd better be calling my mother."

I called, with her standing beside me, listening to what was said. Mother was slightly testy, even before I broke the big news. "Well!" she said. "I was wondering what had become of you."

"We're on our way to Ocean City."

" 'We'? Does that mean Sonya is with you?"

"She's right here, beside me."

"Well at least you took my advice."

"But that's not all. You ready for a surprise?"

". . . All right. What is it?"

She sounded a little grim, but I made myself plow on. "We're getting married, Mother. Monday."

It was quite a while before she said anything, and I began to wonder if she'd fainted or something—the second stunned reaction I'd gotten over the phone that day. But at last she asked: "Did you say married, Gramie?"

"That's right —M-A-Double-R-I-E-D"

"Are you sure you know what you're doing?"

"I think so. Yes, of course."

"I don't think so, Gramie."

"Listen, she's a very nice girl, and we met long before now—around Christmastime, actually. Listen, we're getting married. Who's—"

"Gramie, it has nothing to do with her."

"Then who else can it have to do with?"

That got another long silence, and then: "Gramie, is she there? Can she hear what you're saying to me?"

"She's standing right here beside me."

"I think I should say something to her."

I wasn't so keen about that, because if she started trying to talk Sonya out of it, it would just mean one awful headache. But not letting her talk would have meant a headache almost as bad, so I passed the receiver to Sonya, who started talking herself, without waiting for Mother. She said, "Mrs. Stu, I've seen you a hundred times, in church and kinds of places, and once was presented to you, after a school entertainment, at University Park Elementary, when I played a piano piece." And then, very excited: "Yes, that's right! That's just what I played! And to think you've remembered!"

She talked along, and Mother talked along, and then I took the phone once more. "Well?" said Mother. "Was I all right? I wished her all happiness. Did I please her?"

"She's pinching herself."

"I met her once and liked her."

"She certainly seems to like *you.*"

"Gramie, now that I've collected my wits and pieced it together a bit, it makes more sense than I realized—if you're taking her to New York, to have the surgery done, if that's what you have in mind. And yet—"

"Well, say it! What's your mysterious objection?"
"I can't say it! Not with her standing there!"
"You act like I had a past or something."
"If you haven't a past, that's what frightens me."
"You make it clear like mud in a wineglass."
"When are you having it done?"
"Monday, by the deputy clerk in Rockville."
"Am I invited?"
"Well I hope to tell you you are."
"You'll keep me posted on the details?"
"I certainly will, you bet."

When she'd hung up, Sonya kept studying me. "What's with her?" she asked me. "She seems to like me, she *said* she liked me, and yet something about it is bugging her."

"Well after all, she's my mother."
"Are you promised to somebody else?"
"Not even slightly, no."
"Well there's *something*."
"Listen, I'm her Sonny-Boy. Isn't that enough?"
"I guess."

The Pocohontas is beyond the honkey-tonks, up the beach where the boardwalk ends, and I spotted it by the neon sign on top. But when I pulled in to the parking lot, she made me sit in the car with her, while she made herself up once more, twisting her hair into a knot, pulling the wig over it, and marking her face again with the pencil she had in her bag, or "liner" as she called it. Then at last she said, "Okay," and I handed her out, getting the bags out of the trunk, and locking the car. She preceded me to the desk, wearing the little spring coat, which was beige in color, and walking in a way that seemed strange, heavy on her heels, as though she were slightly tired, without a trace of her usual hop-skip-and-jump. She looked like a woman of thirty, and the clerk never once doubted her. He was all smiles for us both, and gave me the card to sign, first pushing the pen-stand at me. I wrote:

Mr. & Mrs. Graham Kirby,
College Heights Estates,
Hyattsville, Md.

He blotted it, said, "Okay, Mr. Kirby your suite's on the second floor, facing the sea—I think you'll find it in order. Extra blankets in the lower bureau drawer—if you need anything, call."

Carrying your own bag in a motel is a feature I can't get used to, but if that's how it is, it is. I picked up our two and followed her upstairs. She found our suite and unlocked it, and I took our bags in. She followed and closed the door. I was up tight with the moment I'd dreaded, being alone with her, due to spend the night, and perhaps the rest of my life.

Chapter 9

Did I really dread it as much as I thought? I can't say, but I was so nervous I could hardly speak, as just being around her, to see her and hear her and touch her, excited me more than anything ever had. I watched as she took up kind of a survey, first of the kitchenette, which was at one side of the living room, with a chrome-steel sink, very pretty, and a little electric stove; then of the living room, of the bedroom, and of the bathroom, which was beyond the bedroom. She came back and said, "They're in a row, all four rooms, the little ones on the ends, the big ones in the middle, with windows facing the ocean. I like it. Do you?"

I said I did, and then screwed up my nerve to talk of the night, and how we were going to spend it. I told her: "What we'll do is you take the bedroom, and I'll tuck away here, on one of these pull-down things."

I reached for the turnbuckle that held up one of the beds, but suddenly she burst into tears. "Well what the hell?" I snapped. "What have I done, what is it?"

"I thought you loved me."

"...Well, I guess I do, but—?"

But at that she just wailed like a banshee, with tears squirting out of her eyes, first rocking on her feet, then flopping into a chair, where she buried her face on her sleeve and went on with the crying jag. I snapped, "Hey, cool it! And answer me what I asked you: What have I done?"

"Putting me in by myself."

"Well where do you think you should go?"

"With you, of course."

"Are you nuts?"

"Listen, I'm going to be your wife!"

"But you can't sleep with me now—not in your condition. You were the one that said it, it would just be messy. We have to wait till Tuesday."

"I know it, but I could be with you!"

"I'd give my eye teeth to be with you, but—"

"And I could inhale how you smell."

"That sets me nutsier than anything."

"And me nutsiest of all—but I want it."

She wept a bit more, then mentioned that the bedroom had twin beds, "Which won't help much," I said.

Then, wailing, she said: "But I was hoping you'd protect me."

"From what? *Nobody* knows we're here."

"From what's going to happen to me."

"But nothing's going to happen to you."

"Oh yes, something is."

What she was talking about I hadn't the faintest idea, but I had a pretty good idea it wasn't about anything—that it was just a bugaboo she'd made up, to make me say yes, that we'd stay in the bedroom together. By then I was kneeling beside her, first patting her, then giving her little slaps on the cheek, which she didn't seem to mind. Then she rubbed her cheek against mine and smeared me with her tears. Then she kissed me. Then she took off the wig, unpinned the knot of hair on top of her head and let the curls fall on my face. Then she poked a hole in them with her finger and kissed me through the hole. Then she got up, put her bag on a chair, and said: "I put two nighties in, one fresh back from the laundry, the other, the one I slept in all week. Which one do you want me to wear?"

"The one you slept in all week."

"I thought you would."

She took both bags into the bedroom and undressed, so she was naked, but without turning on the light. Then she opened her bag and took out a nightie, holding it out to me. I smelled it and she put it on. She whispered: "I'm glad you like how I smell. I love how *you* smell, Mr. Kirby. Get undressed. But don't put pajamas on yet. I want to smell under your arms."

"Sonya, you're making it tough."

"I love you, that's why."

I undressed down to my underpants, and she came and sniffed my chest, sliding around to my armpit. I said: "That'll do, that has to be all." She stepped back and I got my pajamas out, peeling off price tags and labels. I slipped out of my underpants, then put them on. She stood watching, then turned down a bed and got in it. I turned down the other and got in it. She came over and slipped into bed beside me. I said: "Know what's going to happen to you?"

"You're kissing me nice, that's what."

"That's right, and the——!"

I kissed her, doubled up my legs, put both feet on her bottom, and pushed her out on the floor. "Well that's nice," she said; "I'll say it is, *that's nice.*"

"You *git!* You git in your own bed."

She knelt by her bed and bawled even louder than she had in the sitting room. I said: "You can howl your head off and you don't get back in this bed. Keep it up and I'll blister your backside."

She kept it up.

I rolled out of bed and blistered her.

She stopped howling, sniffled, and said: "Okay—now that I know you love me."

I don't figure that one out.

We lay there some little time, she in her bed, I in mine, her hand occasionally finding my hand, where it lay outside the covers, and patting it. She excited me though, just having her there in the dark near me, and it seemed impossible I'd ever drop off. I must have, though, because suddenly I came wide awake, from some kind of scream in my ear. When it came again, I realized it was from her. Then I realized she was dreaming. I jumped up, shook her, and then shook her again. She woke up, saying: "Oh! Oh! Oh!"

I whispered: "Easy does it, you're having a dream."

"Oh! . . . I told you, didn't I?"

"Is that what you were afraid of?"

"I have that dream every night, that same horrible one. I'm in Prince Georges General Hospital, in the delivery room, giving birth. I have awful pain, but the child comes at last—it's over. Then the nurse is going to bring it, but I say I don't want to see it. But she says I have to, it's the rules. And then she brings it, squirming around and covered with blood. And it's a gorilla."

She called it *goriller.*

I told her: "Now, now, now! Calm down—it was only a dream, and I'm here. Go to sleep—there won't be any gorilla, they're taking it from you Tuesday. Then it'll all be over. So, relax."

"Okay, I'm trying to."

"You're a sweet, wonderful child."

"Now we can go back to sleep."

After a long time her breathing slowed, then got deeper, so I knew she'd fallen asleep. I went back to my bed, but didn't sleep right away. I kept thinking about what it meant, in under her little jokes, about food, about her father's dumbness, about the love my blistering proved, to have this thing inside her. And if I had been chosen, as the instrument of her deliverance, I felt I was consecrated, somehow.

Chapter 10

When I woke up the sun was shining in, and when I looked she was sitting there, in the chair, all dressed, in plaid shorts, blouse, red socks, and tennis shoes, the wig on, her face made up, and wobbling her finger at me.

I said "Good morning" and she said "Haya," and when I asked what time it was, she said eight-fifteen. I said I'd get up if she'd take herself off, but refused to do it with her sitting there. She asked: "But aren't you taking a bath? Don't you want me to scrub your back?"

I said I could scrub my own back, and that she could wait in the lobby, "where I'll join you all in due time." To my surprise she agreed, and went.

I got up, shaved, bathed, and dressed, and when I went down, found her next to the dining room door, waiting. I thanked her for being so sensible, and she said: "Okay, but I'm hungry." I once said she was born hungry, and she said, "You're only young once."

So we went in and ordered, and she had melon, cornflakes, three fried eggs and bacon, toast and coffee—

but I loved watching her eat. I had my usual, orange juice, two eggs and bacon, toast, and coffee.

When we were done I said, "So! Let's get our shopping done, your wedding dress, engagement ring, wedding ring, and beach outfit—so long as we have an ocean, we ought to do something about it." I also thought: The more we sit by the sea, the more we don't sit in that suite, hankering to do things we're not permitted to do.

So we strolled out on the boardwalk, walked down a few steps, came to a shop with clothes in the window, went in, and began buying her stuff. For a wedding dress, she picked out a white linen suit, with white hat, white gloves, white shoes, white stockings, and white bag—and the woman who waited on us, the proprietress as it turned out, found a yard of lace, white lace twelve inches wide, for a veil. Sonya borrowed needle and thread, and "tacked" it, as she called it, to the hat. Then she tried it on and crumpled me up by how she looked, the veil over her face. Then she took the hat off and pinned the veil up, so she could wear it without the veil showing, and at the same time drop it down whenever she wanted, just by pulling the pins. The lady packed the whole outfit into a box that she did up in ribbons.

Then we went on to beachwear. Sonya picked out a bikini, yellow with red lacing, yellow beach shoes, and a red beach cap. Then for me she picked out blue trunks, beach shoes, and a duck hat. Then I picked out robes for us both, and a beach blanket. That all called for another box, so then we had two, one for her to carry, one for me. It all came to $275, and I gave the woman a check, first showing my credit card. She disappeared to phone, though what she'd find out I couldn't think, as it was Saturday and the bank would be closed. But it turned out she had her own system. We heard her call Information and ask for my number. Then we heard her say: "Yes, both numbers, please"—and realized that for free she'd found out I was listed as Graham Kirby, Residence, and Graham Kirby, Inc., Real Estate—a pretty good credit reference.

She came back all smiles and put my check in the register. We asked for a jewelry store, and she directed us to one.

But then annoyance set in. Sonya picked out two rings, one for our engagement, a diamond solitaire, and a wedding ring, platinum with chasing cut in it. The tab was a bit over $1,000, but the jeweler shook his head. "Sir," he said, "your card entitles you to five hundred dollars' credit, but beyond that it's Saturday and I have no way to check—the amount is too large for me to take a chance on. Monday, if you'll come in, I'm sure we can work something out."

I drew breath to explode, but Sonya said: "Please, please, forget it—they have jewelry stores in Rockville, and we can pick up my rings there."

As we went trudging back to the motel, I was growling like a bear, and she joined in in her own way: "He's a bastard, a creep, and a crumb, but let's not let him ruin our day." Pretty soon, not wanting to, I had to laugh, and we were happy again. When we arrived once more in our suite, I opened the box full of things, and we went in the bedroom to dress.

She made it touch, of course, parading around with no clothes on, and laughing at me when I turned my back to put on my trunks. Still, she got into her bikini, hat, and shoes, and I got into my trunks, shoes, and hat, and both of us put on our robes. Then I picked up our beach bag and blanket, and we went downstairs. Beach clothes are allowed in Ocean City lobbies, not in Atlantic City or Rehoboth. We left our key at the desk and went out to the beach. It was filling with people and the guards were coming on duty, as it was after twelve o'clock. We had forgotten a beach umbrella, but the boardwalk cast a shadow and we sat in it awhile, first spreading the beach blanket. Then she wanted to sunbathe, so we moved out in the glare.

"Now," she said, "you have to rub me with lotion, and then of course I'll rub you." She had taken a bottle from the beach bag and handed it to me. So with her, if it wasn't one thing it was something else, and with her pointing to all sorts of intimate places, and saying: "No, not up and down, *circular*." And the thoroughness with which she rubbed me was really a thing to remember.

Pretty soon I said: "I think it's time we went in."

"Back? To the room? So soon?"

"To the ocean. For a swim."

"Oh! Then okay."

We kicked off our beach shoes, and I tossed my hat on the blanket. Then we went hand-in-hand to the surf, which was just the least bit high, as a sea breeze was coming in. But she was expert at going through it. First, she waited until a wave smashed down at her feet, then waded out in the wash to brace for the next one, standing sidewise, her arms in the air. But she was just a bit further out than the spot where it would crest, so when it came it rocked her, but didn't smash her down. As soon as it passed she leveled out and started to swim. By the time the next one came, she was out past the whitecaps. I did exactly as she did, not too successfully, alas. One comber knocked me down, and I was a minute or two getting out to where she was swimming. She grabbed my hand and gave it a shake. Then she started swimming with me, side by side.

First we swam with trudgen strokes, then on our backs, floating. It gives you a funny sensation, as all you can feel is the lift of the swells, as they raise you and lower you down, and all you can see is the sky.

She looked up, pointed, and asked: "See that?"

". . . That cloud?"

"Cloud nine – where we'll be Tuesday night."

"It's quite a handsome cloud."

"Mr. Kirby, I could be happy with you."

". . . Tuesday will tell the tale."

"Could you be happy with me?"

"We can cross that bridge when we come to it."

"I'm'n do my best to make you."

That's what she said, *I'm'n,* meaning, I suppose, "I'm going to."

I told her: "All's fair in love or war."

"That's it, I'm'n *try*."

We began swimming again, still on our backs, but headed out to sea, and the further we went, the longer the swells got, and the smoother they were. It was us and the sea and the sky, as though she and I were suspended in wet eternity. I thought about God, the second time I had, around her. Then cutting the air came a whistle. She cocked her head up, waved, and blew a kiss. I turned in time to see the lifeguard blowing a kiss, and waving at her to come in. I asked: "Since when did you get so chummy with *him?"*

"Oh he's cute."

"And when did this intimacy start?"

"He was watching, while you were smearing me up."

"Observant little cuss."

We swam in, and at a certain point she looked behind her. Then she stretched out flat, and she rode it as though on a surfboard. It carried her in to the sand, where she dug in with her hands and then pulled her feet up. Then she was staggering clear.

I tried to copycat, and got washed a few feet toward shore. I stood up only to be smashed down on my face, in a mix of gravel and water, as a wave flattened me. I stood up and it happened again. Next thing I knew, she had me by the hand and was pulling me out.

"You're *fighting* it—you mustn't do that. You have to go along with it."

"I'll remember that, next time."

"We better shower, before the salt cakes on."

She put on her shoes, put mine on me, and rolled up the beach blanket. When we climbed up on the boardwalk, the guard was disagreeable to her. "Hey, smart guy," he called, "There's sharks out there, you know."

"Oh, they're nothing but fish."

She tossed it off very saucy, and if there was any trace of the twenty-five-year-old woman, with slightly graying hair, that she had been the night before, I couldn't see it myself. In her red cap and yellow-and-red bikini, she looked like what she was, a sixteen-year-old brat with a shape to write home about.

"That's right," the lifeguard said, "but they're hungry fish, and the thing they'rc fondest of is a good-looking chick, all white meat."

"Oh my, you're making me nervous."

"I hope I'm getting through."

"Okay, now I know."

"Dad, can I date her up?"

". . . Well, that would be up to her."

"*What do you mean, up to me?*" She ripped it, in a kind of a scream. And then, to him: "He's not inny Dad, he's my husband!"

"You got to be putting me on!"

"You heard me, *my husband!*"

We put on our beach robes, and I heard him mumble, "Is that a lucky son of a bitch." We went in the lobby, picked up our key at the desk, and went on up to the suite. We were hardly inside when she yelled: "Is that all I mean to you? That it's up to me if I date?"

"That's all – date any time you please."

"Well thanks. I'll remember that."

"Date and stay dated, for good!"

"And what's that supposed to mean?"

"Means that guy didn't ask for a date, all on his own think-up—he got encouragement, plenty."

"Says who?"

"Goddam it, I saw you blow him a kiss!"

"You call that encouragement?"

"What do you call it, for instance?"

I guess there was more, anyway till she had the beach robe off, and slipped out of her bathing suit. I fired one at her bottom that went off like a pistol shot. She laughed, wrapped me in her arms and kissed me. When we went in the bedroom it was all done up, and my five dollars, that I'd left for the maid, was gone. "Okay," I said, "let's wash off the salt—then get dressed. In separate rooms."

Her answer was to unbuckle the belt of my trunks, strip them off, and pull off my shoes. That left us with nothing on, except that she still wore her cap. She laughed and sicked her finger at me, especially my male anatomy. She had told me quite a few times "we had it in sex education," and yet it seemed to excite her, partly I think from plain adolescent curiosity.

I said: "All right, let's get it over with," and she took me by the hand, leading me to the bathroom.

She led me to the tub, and when we had both stepped in, dropped the shower curtains and pulled them together. Then she turned on the water and adjusted to medium hot. Then, standing belly-to-belly with me, she held her face up, letting the water pour over it. "Nice?" she asked.

"Would be, if it was Tuesday."

"It's only three days off."

"Only? *Only?*"

She dropped her head to my chest, and we stood there a long time, like Adam and Eve in the Garden. Then at last she turned off the water, took a towel, and dried me off, with care—a little too much care, I thought. Taking another towel, she dried herself off, and if you think I got out of the tub, you're wrong. I just stood there, drinking her in. She was painstaking and thorough, in all kinds of intimate places, at last putting a foot on the side of the tub, to give it proper attention. She said: "First one little tootsie, then the other little—"

But she never finished. The other foot slipped and she fell, in a loud flub-a-dub crash. I was over her in a second, lifting her, asking: "Little Sonya, are you all right? Are you hurt?"

"No, no! I'm all right!"

"Lock your fingers back of my neck, so I can lift you!"

She did and I raised her up, so she could stand with me, still in the tub. "Are you all right?" I asked again.

"Yes."

But then: "Something's happened inside."

"Hold everything."

I lifted her, got one foot outside the tub, then the other foot, still holding her, but almost slipping myself. Then I carried her into the bedroom, turned down the covers on her bed, and eased her down on it. "Get me a towel," she whispered. "I'm bleeding."

I got the towel, tucked it under her, and picked up the phone, ready to tear the place apart to get a doctor there, quick. But I didn't have to do any tearing—a doctor had offices right there, and when the girl found out what the trouble was, she said: "The doctor will be there in just a few minutes."

"What's his name?"

"Sandoval."

I hung up and we stared in each other's eyes. "I think you've aborted," I said.

"I'm sure I have."

We stared at each other again, I so excited I couldn't talk. But she looked away, closed her eyes, and started to cry, sad, hopeless crying, with little shakes of her shoulders, as she held her hands to her face.

Chapter 11

It made no sense to me, but she kept on, while I tried to figure it out. And in spite of my fighting it back, a suspicion entered my mind. I mean, if she had aborted, if this was what we thought, why was she crying about it? And why didn't she turn to me, instead of including me out? And if she was crying because it was gone, that thing she had inside, what meaning did that have, in regard to all the rest? Was she actually raped, did she find Burl repugnant, and was this marriage all an act?

But when I got that far with it, she suddenly burst out: "Give me my wig! It's in the top bureau drawer!"

I did, and she pulled it on. Then she grabbed her bag from the night table, took out the liner, and marked up her face once more. She was barely down when a knock came on the sitting room door, and I opened it to let in the doctor, a young guy, with kind of a Spanish look and the usual zipper satchel.

I said my wife had had an accident, and took him into the bedroom. Then I left him alone with her, so she could do her own talking, apparently giving details. I heard him go to the bathroom and come back, and then pretty soon he came out, into the room with me, and closed the door.

I said, "What do I owe you, Doctor?"

"Twenty-five dollars, please."

I wrote the check, then asked: "What next? I mean, do I have to take her to a hospital? And if so, which is the nearest one?"

"She's in luck. Hospital's not indicated."

"Well, give. What happened?"

"She lost the child, that's all. But she aborted clean—foetus and placenta were both there, on the towel. When the placenta doesn't come, there has to be a curettage. However, it did come, and that's it. The bleeding has stopped, but I packed her with gauze, which she can take out whenever she wants."

"You greatly relieve my mind."

"I also gave her a hypo."

"You mean, she's in pain?"

"No—so she can sleep. It's an awful shock, it jangles the hell out of them." He hesitated, then went on: "They take it in various ways—some want nothing to do with the husband for weeks—others take it opposite: they want him at once, it's the one thing that calms them down. How she'll feel I don't know, and you shouldn't force yourself on her. But if she *should* feel in the humor, don't withhold it from some mistaken idea of duty. What she wants is what she should have."

"I'll remember what you say."

He picked up his check and left, and I tiptoed in to her, hoping to find a change, now that she knew for certain what we'd been guessing at, so she'd be in a different humor. But she was crying again, and wouldn't look at me. "Hey!" I said, shaking her. "What is this? What are you crying about? Didn't he tell you? It's what we thought—you miscarried. It's all over, it's what we've been praying for! You won't have that dream anymore, we don't have to go to New York!"

"And you don't have to marry me!"

". . . Is that what's been bugging you?"

"It's enough, isn't it?"

My mouth was trying to say she was just being silly, but the words wouldn't come. Actually, it was the first I'd thought of that angle, and somehow, now that she'd brought it up, it didn't seem silly at all. I swallowed a couple of times, then told her: "Listen, one thing at a time, let's cross that bridge when we come to it. The main thing is, you're rid of that horrible thing that's been making your life hell. Now, get yourself some sleep, and then we'll take it from there. Decide what we're going to do."

"Don't you ever cross that bridge?"

"I said one thing at a time."

"You're always talking about it."

"Can't we talk when you're yourself?"

"I'm myself now. I'm always myself."

I left her, went down to the boardwalk, and headed across to the beach. As I passed the guard called down:"I'm sorry, sir, if I mistook the young lady for your daughter."

"It's okay, most people do."

"I meant what I said about sharks—they're out there, and they don't always give notice by shoving a fin out of water. Sometimes they shoot up from below and help themselves to a bite. Sharks are nothing to fool with."

"I'll see that she stays closer in."

I climbed down to the sand, found a small dune, and sat down, facing the sea. Then I tried to think. I told myself: "Now that you don't have to, now that there's no real need, you must be out of your mind, even considering marrying this girl, this teenage child, whom you barely knew until yesterday. It's over—the crisis is passed. You've done the right thing, or at least you were willing to. Now, take her home and let her go on with her life—as what she is, a schoolgirl—and forget any idea you had of going further with it. No doubt she'll suffer a bit, but she'll get over it, and better have the break now, with no great damage done, than later, as utter disaster."

That seemed to cover it, and for a time I sat there, under the illusion the thing was settled. Then I thought: "But now that you're threshing it out, it wouldn't hurt at all to talk it over with someone, especially the one person you're close to, who's smart on all such things."

I climbed up the boardwalk again, walked down to a drugstore and called Mother. The phone rang and rang and rang, but then who answered, in a snappish, disaggreeable way, wasn't Mother but Burl.

I hung up without saying a word.

I went back to my dune and sulked at her. I thought: "You did tell her, that's true, that you were getting married, and that ended the situation, so she had no further reason for keeping that rat under cover, but did she have to bring him in the house, within hours of the time I talked to her?" It turned out later she did, for a reason quite different from any I thought she had, but I didn't know that then, and sat there for quite a while, feeling sorry for myself.

Then I got to thinking about my life, especially the other girls in it. There hadn't been too many, call it two or three, beginning with the one I had had in college, who lived at the Taft Hotel, and would sneak out on weekends, when I'd drive her to Milford or Norwalk or Bridgeport, and we'd shack up at some motel. But her people moved to Boston, and though she hinted around about marriage, I wasn't ready for it, and she passed out of my life. Then, after I started in business, I bumped into this girl in

Baltimore, who worked in a TV station, and had an apartment on Charles Street. It was okay, but then her hours got switched, so it all got too complicated, and then we didn't date any more.

Later, after I moved to College Heights Estates, there was a woman who showed houses for me. You have a house for sale, you put a woman in it Sundays, and she shows it to whoever comes. So my houses, for reasons I'll explain, generally sell pretty quick, and she had a nice thing going. She was a widow up in her thirties, a bit on the plump side, but pretty, and always beautifully dressed. One night when I took her her check, she asked if I'd like to come in, and when I did, put out Scotch.

The rest was almost on cue—the pass, the brush, the brush of the brush, the peeling off in her bedroom. From there on in, we ran on kind of a schedule, except for one odd thing: After that one time, she never asked me to her place. She always came to mine, in her little Chevy, and after a cocktail, love, and dinner, drove home again, always around eight o'clock. And then one day she rang, to say she'd just been married. It turned out then that she'd been engaged all along, to a rich, middle-aged guy, whose mother was at death's door, and who until it happened didn't feel himself free. While he was marking time he was too decent to make passes at her, which left her with certain desires. And so, I'd come in handy.

That hadn't been too long ago, and I sat thinking about her, about the girl in New Haven, and about the one in Baltimore. I'd been quite close to each one, and yet none of them had rocked me as Sonya had, in the twenty-four hours I had known her. And all of a sudden what had seemed to be settled wasn't any more. I began wondering what this girl had that the others hadn't had. And I heard my own voice answer: "Brains, for one thing. Maybe she's just a schoolgirl, but she was the one, just the same, who figured out what could be done to mop up that awful mess." That, I have to admit, put things in a different light. I sat there some more, with the breeze freshening up, and the surf really starting to talk. I thought of our swim out to sea, with her hand in mine, giving me courage. I thought how we'd looked at Cloud Nine and what she had said.

Then I heard my own voice again: "Another thing about her: When you're with her you think about God."

I knew then I was going to marry her.

I went in, and to give her more time to sleep, had some dinner in the dining room. When I went up it was just after seven, though of course, with daylight saving, still broad day outside. I opened the door real quiet, expecting to tiptoe into the bedroom and see if she'd come awake. But there she was, dressed, in the clothes she'd had on yesterday, stuffing things into her bag which was on a chair. On another chair was a hatbox, which was open, the new hat in it. But there hadn't been any hatbox, which meant she must have gone out, after I went to the beach, and bought one. I wondered how much of a hypo it was, but said nothing about it, asking: "Well? Where do you think you're going?"

"Home," she snapped.

"Some particular *reason?*"

"You're not wanted you take yourself off."

"Somebody *say* you weren't wanted?"

"Good as. At least they made it plain."

"I just don't seem to recall it."

"Oh for Christ sake, Mr. Kirby, will you knock it off with the blibber-blabber? Yeah, you said it—you couldn't look me in the eye, and that's saying it, plain as it can be said."

"When was this?"

"I said quit cracking dumb!"

I stood watching her, not knowing what to say, because

of course, it was true, what she was dishing out, and you hate to own up to what makes you look crummy. However, this was the nitty-gritty, and no time for ducking and dodging. Finally I said: "Okay, I own up, I gave you a stall before, after the doctor left. I wanted to think things over, which I'd had no chance to do, up until then, at all. And if you think I apologize for it, you're damned well mistaken. I wanted to think it over and did think it over, plenty."

"Oh my, the Thinker, by Rodin."

She called him *Rodang.*

"Did you hear what I said?"

"My bus leaves at nine o'clock."

"Well it's not yet eight, so you have plenty of time. If you've got that much straight, that I did think it over, I'll get on to the next thing."

"You mean that bridge that never gets crossed?"

"So happens we're crossing it now."

"Oh no we're not, I'm leaving."

"First thing: I don't have to marry you."

"You're telling me? *You're telling me?*"

"Sonya, have you got that much straight?"

"Do you want me to scream or what?"

"But I'm going to."

"Going to what?"

"Marry you, what do you think?"

"You and who else?"

"Did you hear me?"

"I ain't deaf. . . When?"

"Why not now?"

"Who would marry us now? We don't even have a license!"

"Someone could be found."

She looked me up and down, and I went on: "They're right here in this room, everyone we need. Because when two people get married, who does it is *them.* The rest of it, the license, the service, the preacher, the clerk, is all for the law and the record. What's for God, *they* do. 'With this ring I thee wed,' he tells her, and she swears to love, honor, and obey'—and you better obey, brat. As you know, I don't have any ring, but I do have something else, something you've admired, and—"

"Then, I'll think about it."

"Then, suppose you get the hell out!"

Because I was wrought up too, more than I'd realized, and for some reason she riled me. As I spoke I kicked her square in the bottom, so hard she plunged and fell. Then horror swept over me, at what it might do to her, after what had happened before, and I dropped to my knees in front of a chair, whispering: "Dear God, don't let it be that she's hurt!"

But then she was there beside me, her arm on my shoulder pulling me, pulling me close and whispering: "Don't take on like that, please, please, please! I love it when you bop me—and that was a dilly, a real boot in the tail. Okay, I thought about it! I'm willing, I'm ready! Okay, wed me—wed me nice, wed me!"

Chapter 12

I wedded her. I wedded her and kept on wedding her—that night, the next day, which was Sunday, and the next night. Some of those weddings lasted an hour, when time stood still, and we didn't care if it ever got going again. Often, she would be topside, her head on my shoulder, whispering: "I'm not asleep, I've got my eyes open, I'm enjoying the view, up here from Cloud Nine. It's so pretty you can't believe it—things I've never seen, except on TV sometimes, horses and sheep and cows, and chickens running around. Ducks too, but I *have* seen them, flying over, V-shape. And flowers, red ones, white ones, and blue ones, all kinds of beautiful flowers. And trees, gray big trees, and bushes. And grass, green grass that smells like you...Now, *you're* on our cloud, looking up. What do *you* see?"

"Stars."

"Are they pretty?"

"Beautiful."

"There's just one thing."

"Yes, little Sonya. What is it?"

"This cloud is shaped like a bubble chair. Suppose something made it go *pop*. What would happen to us?"

"We'd go *bump*."

"That wouldn't be so good."

"We can't let it happen, ever."

"That's it. It's up to us, Mr. Kirby."

"There's one other thing, too."

". . . Yeah? What's that?"

"*Must* you call me Mr. Kirby?"

"You mean, now that we're married?"

"Yes, that's what I mean, of course."

"Or arc we?"

"I thought that was settled."

"Then – what does your mother call you?"

"Gramie."

"Would you like me to call you that?"

"I'd love it."

"I'll practice up, in my mind."

So she practiced up, in her mind, and then one time, in a flaming moment, whispered: "Gramie!" That did it, and from then on she seemed like a wife. I began telling her things, bragging I guess, like my system for selling houses. "I lose three listings out of ten," I explained to her, "from being so tough, and as some say, so dictatorial. But – the other seven I sell fast. And what makes me so objectionable? I won't list a house unless the owner agrees to accept a reasonable price. That's the trouble selling houses, you list it and list it and advertise it on Sundays, for months, simply because of a dream price they think they can get, just by holding out. I jar them loose from that dream. I tell them: 'Come off it! I know what your house will bring – it's my business to know and I do. But if you don't believe me, put an appraiser on it, put your own appraiser on it, and what he comes up with I'll accept. I'm an appraiser myself, but if he says I'm nuts okay—find yourself another agent.' As a rule they listen to me, but three out of ten don't, and I lose 'em. But the ones I don't lose are making me the most successful broker in Hyattsville."

"I always heard you were."

"Kiss your famous husband."

And finally, the second night, when she was lying close in my arms, I told her about the Dream. She listened as I lined it out: "The whole farm, Jane Sibert's sixty seven acres, I mean to chop into one-acre lots, big places, estates, and write it into the deed, that I approve exterior plans. It's how you do, in an exclusive development, to make sure it doesn't run down, that pikers don't build on the cheap—it's how they do in Malibu Beach, Williamsburg, and all places that really have class. And I'll approve nothing but Southern mansions, with oaks, elms, gum, and magnolias. And that house that Jane Sibert lives in, I'll use it for demonstration, first remodeling, to make it the most Southern mansion of all. I'll peel off that front porch, put a neat little entrance in, and an annex right and left, a rec room and a garage, and—lo and behold—it's Southern something to look at. And that mudhole she calls a drive, that circular thing out front, what am I doing with that? I'm dozing the mud out first, then lining it with bricks—putting brick borders down, inside and outside the loop, and painting them with whitewash. Then, between the two rows of brick I'm filling with oyster shells.

"Everyone's forgotten about them, all they know now is blacktops. But oyster shells are cheaper—there's a place in Washington that sells them, a restaurant on Maine Avenue with a tremendous pile out back—and they're prettier. They're snow white, and they look like Dixie! And in the middle, in the circle that runs around, I'm putting a rose garden in—and then I'll guarantee you, I'll have something they'll come to see."

". . . A rose garden? Why?"

"It's the Dixie flower, that's why. They have them all over the South—even in Mexico. With the roses I'll put across the idea that these are the Dixie Estates!"

"I wouldn't plant 'em, no such."

". . . What wouldn't you plant, then?"

" 'Oh I wish I was in the land of'—*roses?*"

"I see what you mean, *cotton.*"

"Gramie, did you ever see cotton growing?"

"I can't say I have, no."

"I have, and it's beautiful. One summer we went on a trip, my mother and I, to visit her sister, Aunt Sue, who lives in New Orleans. But we drove by way of Paducah, where my father's sister lives, Aunt Annabelle. From Paducah we drove south, along the Mississippi, and all the way down we saw cotton, the prettiest growing thing you ever saw in your life—the leaves are so green, the rows are so even. It was six inches high in Kentucky, ten inches in Tennessee, a foot in Mississippi, and bush-height in Louisiana. But in Louisiana we saw the flowers, big, creamy white ones, that turn red when the sun goes down. Did you know that, Gramie? The second day they're red. But they weren't all.

"Driving back in the early fall we saw the real show. The bushes still had their leaves, but in place of flowers there were bolls, bolls of real cotton, the softest, warmest things you ever saw, just like little bunnies. And they're pure white, the same color as your shells. And wouldn't that be a sight, Gramie, for the Dixie moon to shine on! In the Indian summer, with the shells shining like snow, the cotton bolls shining like silver, and all of it shining like Dixie. And wouldn't that advertise it! And—— "

"It's in, it's an inspiration!"

"And I thought it up? I'm the one?"

"You, beautiful you!"

"And I'm kind of a help to you?"

"You're the best asset I have!"

We lay a long time, inhaling each other, dreaming of moonlight and cotton. And then: "Gramie, why did she do that?"

"Why did who do what?"

"Mrs. Sibert? Why did she put you in her will?"

"I thought I told you: She likes me, and she doesn't have anyone else. And, I kick in with money."

"What will she think about me?"

"She'll love you, as everyone does."

"Who's everyone? Who do you know that loves me?"

". . . I know no reason they wouldn't."

"She could have one, though. *She* could love *you.*"

"Don't be silly."

"I'm not being silly. But maybe she is."

"I'm getting dizzy. In what way would she be silly?"

"About you—I already said."

"I can't imagine such a thing."

"I can, easy as pie."

Chapter 13

It was the first time that subject came up, but wasn't to be the last, as I found out Monday morning, when I called Mother, to find out if she still wanted to come to the wedding. I sent Sonya up to pack as soon as we finished breakfast, and walked on down to the drugstore to use the pay phone. I kept my hand on the hook, to hang up if Burl answered, but who came on was Mother, and I started off pretty peevish. "Okay," I snapped, "I did tell you I meant to get married, and that ended the danger to Burl, but it does seem to me you were rushing things, to bring him back in the house so soon – you must like this rat better than you pretend."

"I don't like him at all."

"Then what was he doing there Saturday when I called?"

"Putting his things in a trunk I let him take, and getting ready to leave. I gave him two hours, and went out – to the movies, actually."

"You mean he's gone?"

"I told you! I kicked him the hell out."

"Well, hooray. I take back everything."

"I'd rather not talk about it, though no doubt I will when I feel myself able. — Is something on your mind?"

"Do you still want to come to my wedding?"

"Wait a minute, wait a minute, wait a minute!"

"Mother, do you or don't you?"

"Gramie, we have to talk about that — the situation has changed, here at home, since you left — especially with the Langs."

"What are they up to *now?*"

"They're not up to anything — at last they've listened to reason. She of course, Mrs. Lang, regards you as a catch, and hates to give you up, but he had completely lost his nerve, and has finally come around to the simple, sensible way of winding the thing up, especially if you bear the expense."

"What *are* you talking about?"

"New York! He's willing to take her there and have the operation done. And so, except for a few hundred dollars, you'll be out from under."

"You mean you engineered all this?"

"Gramie, I love you, I hope I don't let you down."

"But nobody *asked* you to."

"Gramie, you're in a mess. Can't you —— "

"I'm not. It's all over. She aborted."

". . . She — what?"

"Had a miscarriage."

"Oh, thank God! Thank the dear merciful God."

"Yeah, we've been thanking Him too."

"Now, life can go on."

But she said it in a somewhat peculiar way, and I asked her: "What's that supposed to mean? If anything?"

"You don't have to marry this girl."

"No, but I'm going to."

"You're *going* to?"

"Yeah, that's right. Today."

"But why?"

"I want to."

"But don't you know what it's going to cost you?"

I supposed she was alluding to Sonya's age, and the price an older man paid for getting mixed up with a girl, her simple girlish friends, and her simple girlish talk, so I decided to let her say it and then speak my piece about it. I said: "I'll bite, what is it going to cost me?"

"Jane Sibert's farm, is all."

". . . What does *she* have to do with it?"

"Gramie, she loves you, that's what."

"Are you being funny?"

"Gramie, stop playing games with me! Here you've been in this woman's bed, *laying* her, if I have to use plain English, for ten years, and you pretend you don't know how she feels? You think it was just biological with her? A little physical convenience? As it apparently has been to you?"

"I've been *whatting* her?"

"Gramie, I told you stop playing dumb!"

"I don't know what you're talking about."

"You mean to say you haven't been?"

"I mean to say that exactly."

"Then wait a minute, give me a chance to readjust. Gramie, that was the whole idea—not admitted by her, of course, or by me. But you were fifteen years old, and it was time, high time, you stop playing with yourself like Shakespeare and found someone to play with. And she was there and she was cute and she was hot—she wanted you, bad. It's why I let you go. Don't tell me you blew it?"

"It never once entered my mind."

"Oh my, you *are* in trouble."

"Then if I am, she is. I keep her, don't forget. If I don't send her her checks, she doesn't eat. So the situation is negotiable, as they say."

"And I'm in trouble. I've said nothing to you, but I've been selling securities, to buck up my cash reserve, so I'll have money to swing your dream when the time comes. It makes my blood run cold to think how close I am, as I sit here this very minute, to the brink. However, the dream can still be saved. I think you must see now, that you can't throw it away, for the sake of this little snip—"

"Mother, I mean to marry her."

"Oh for God's sake, be your age!"

"I'm trying to be."

"Okay then—if you love her, lay her. But—"

"I mean to marry her."

"Gramie! No! Please!"

"For the last time: Do you want to come to my wedding?"

". . . Have you talked with Jane about it?"

"How would I talk to her? She'd left on her trip, to be gone for a month, before the subject came up. I don't know where she is, to call her, and she doesn't know where I am, here at Ocean City, to call me. So of course I haven't talked with her."

"Couldn't you hold off? Until you do?"

"And say what?"

"Find out how she feels."

"You mean, ask her permission?"

"Gramie, she's entitled to be heard."

"Not on this—nobody is, but me and Sonya."

"Well, thank you!"

"Not even beautiful you—get your mouth out."

"Now I know where I get off."

"Are you coming?"

She went into a long harangue, with tears, pleas, and jokes about Jane's desires, saying everything all over, and when at last I told her to cool it, that my mind was made up, she moaned: "Then—if you're set on doing this thing—of course I want to come. I thought her a very nice child, and I felt she was a musician. Over the phone I liked her—she was respectful, and I felt she had something. So it's not personal. But Gramie: You're talking about love, I'm talking about money—and there's no reason you can't have both. You can have that million dollars, and you can also have love, love by the dark of the moon, that Jane doesn't know about. And once Sonya gets through her head what she eventually will come into, as Jane can't live forever, you'll be surprised at how sensible she'll be. Will you talk it over with *her?* She's entitled to be heard, you said!"

"No, I won't."

"Then all right, I'll come to your wedding."

She made it sound like good-bye in the deathhouse, but I played it straight, thanking her, and said we could meet at the Langs' and all go in my car. Then she asked if it would help if she rode the Langs in her car to Rockville, so I could go there with Sonya, and not have to haul anyone else. I said it would, and that if she would call the Langs, I'd check with her later, as soon as I got home with Sonya.

"Then all right, Gramie. God bless."

"And God bless you, Sweetie Pie."

I walked back up the boardwalk again, but before going upstairs climbed down once more to the sand, and camped again on my dune. The beach was deserted at this hour, except for a girl some distance down, exercising a dog with a ball. It was me, the sand, and the sea, and I thought to myself, Why are you being so noble? I don't think anyone's ever quite sure why he does something important, but my coming back to this dune, to look at the sea and think, was certainly some kind of tip-off. Because once more I thought about God, who was certainly part of it, this decision I had come to. Until now, God and I weren't exactly intimates. I often took Mother to church, and sometimes Jane went with us, to St. Andrews in College Park, and put something in the plate, as well as kicked in for all kinds of different charities but it was strictly a Sunday thing, and I'm not sure I ever prayed. But when I was with Sonya, God was part of it too, and I wasn't sure He'd get the point, or play it funny at all, if I gave Him a ring just now, and said: "Hold everything, God—there's been a switch in the plans, and I don't want to get married now." I thought He might be getting a bit sick of me. I thought, when you make up your mind on something, at least something as big as that, you've made it up for keeps or it's not made up at all. I knew then it would stay made up.

When I got back to the suite, Sonya was charging around, dragging the bags to the door, her suitcase, my canvas zipper bag, the hatbox, and the various other boxes. She said: "Okay, you carry the bag, I'll carry the rest."

"Fine. Kiss me."

"What did she say?"

"What did who say?"

"Your mother. Remember?"

"Oh! That she's hauling your parents to Rockville."

"What else?"

"That she likes you, that she thinks you're a real musician, that though young, she felt you had something, when she talked to you over the phone."

"What else?"

"Was I sure I knew what I was doing."

"And what did you say to *that?*"

"That I was."

"And what did she say to *that?*"

"I told you: She's hauling your parents to Rockville."

She kissed me, but gave me a squinty look.

Chapter 14

For the rest of the morning, things went nice for us. We stopped in Salisbury, where I bought flowers, corsages for the ladies, boutonnieres for Mr. Lang and me, and while they were being done up, rings for Sonya, at a jewelry store a few steps from the florist. I got her a sapphire solitaire engagement ring that cost more than I want to say, and a platinum wedding ring, a chased band with our initials engraved inside, in such a way as to intertwine. All that they did while we waited, and took my cheek without even calling up about it.

Sonya was pleased as a child with a rattle, and held the sapphire up for the sunlight to catch it, all during the drive home. We arrived around twelve-thirty, running into no delay on the bridge, and left the flowers in the car while she went to change to her wedding dress. I followed with the bags, and unzipped her and started to peel her. However, she pushed me aside and sat down in the armchair, there in the master bedroom. "Gramie," she said, "one thing a sixteen-year-old knows, better than other people, because she does it so often herself, is when someone is lying. And you've been lying to me, ever since you came back from that call, the one put in to your mother. So I ask you, I ask you once more: What did she say?"

"Sonya, I've told you."

"Call me a cab."

"... Cab? What for?"

"Go home."

"I thought we were getting married."

"We were. Now I'm not."

I sat down on the bed and tried to think. Pretty soon I said, "She asked about Jane Sibert."

"In what way, asked about her?"

"Did I realize she likes me."

"She loves you, is that what she meant?"

Then, one word at a time, jerky and quick, I gave her the whole bit, what Mother had said, what I had said, without holding anything back. She said: "What she thought is what we thought, *all* of us."

"Who is we?"

"Us kids?"

"That I was sleeping with her?"

"Well? It's what your mother thought too."

"Seems that everyone thought it but me."

"Are you sure you didn't?"

"Who knows if I don't."

"You know if you're telling the truth? Gramie, she's not so old, and she had her mind on you, that we all could see. So you must have let her have it! You—"

"Well goddam it, I didn't!"

"Okay, then you didn't."

She got up, went to the window, and stood looking out. Then she zipped up her dress, the one I'd been taking off. Then she sat down on the bed, picked up the phone, and ordered a cab. Then she unzipped my bag, and switched her nighties to her bag. I reached over, picked up the phone, and cancelled the cab order. She sat down with me, kissed me, and said: "Gramie, it cannot be, we'd just be doomed, we'd be doomed, right from the start. No girl is worth a million dollars."

"You're worth a hundred million."

At that she started to cry, and buried her face on my shoulder. Then, between sobs: "No, I'm not—and not worth *this* million dollars—which is all hooked up with a dream—about shells and cotton and moonlight."

"There's just one thing."

". . . Yes, Gramie, what is it?"

"That kick in the tail——?"

"No, please, I couldn't say no to *that!*"

She ranted on, pleading with me, "not to make it so hard for me—so hard to keep my promise—didn't I say, didn't I say it, Gramie, that I wouldn't be inny pest?" And then, whispering: "Gramie, there's not inny need for us to get married. Because we could see each other. She wouldn't have to know, Mrs. Sibert I'm talking about. We could meet, on the Q.T.——"

"And do it?"

"Yes! On our same beautiful Cloud Nine."

"By a funny coincidence, that's what Mother suggested."

"Oh, she's sweet! So we're going to——?"

"Stand up!"

". . . What for?"

"So I can kick your beautiful tail."

"You mean I have to get married?"

"Yes."

"Okay."

We got to Rockville at five of two, and the others were waiting for us, out on the courthouse lawn, Mother in dark red, the color she likes best, Mrs. Lang in gray, Mr. Lang in a dark suit. When I got out of the car, I carried three boxes, two of the ladies' corsages, one of Mr. Lang's carnation. I was wearing mine, and Sonya was wearing her corsage of orange blossoms they dug up in Salisbury. We all stood around for a minute, helping each other pin up, and then went inside, where they were ready for us. The lady who had sold us our license was nicely turned out in pink, and the two girls in the office, who stood up with us as witnesses, were in pretty summer dresses, but I don't recollect which color. Mr. Lucas, the deputy clerk who read the service, had on a mixed gray summer suit, very dignified.

Mr. Lang gave the bride away, and of course I fumbled the ring. I knew where I'd put it, where I *thought* I'd put it, in my coat pocket, but when I reached for it it wasn't there.

"Take your time," said Mr. Lucas soothingly. "It really wouldn't be legal if the groom didn't lose the ring."

Then I found it, in the *other* coat pocket. Then we were all sitting down, while the girls signed the certificate, and Mother said: "Sonya, Gramie has everything to make music with, in that living room of his, every mechanical thing, to work when a button is pushed – except something you work yourself. Would you like a piano from me? As a wedding present I mean."

"Oh, Mrs. Stu! Oh!"

Sonya started to cry, then kissed Mother. Mrs. Lang said: "We have something in mind, Sonya. We'll give you a present too."

"We don't aim to be skunked."

At Mr. Lang's remark we laughed, as usual.

Then at last, around four, we were home, Sonya with the veil pinned up, but without her corsage, as she tossed it to one of the girls, the one who came up with a handful of rice to throw at us, as we sailed down the courthouse steps. I unlocked the door, put the bags inside, and picked Sonya up in my arms. Mrs. Persoff, who lives next door, was cutting peonies in her garden, and suddenly stopped and stared. “Yes!” I called to her. “It’s what you think! Congratulate me!”

She dropped her shears and clapped her hands, and Sonya blew her a kiss. I carried her in. “Okay,” I said, still not putting her down. “Frog turned into a prince—three wishes coming to you, say what they’re going to be!”

“I want to be carried upstairs.”

I carried her up. “What next?”

“I want to be flopped on that bed.”

I flopped her. “One more?”

“I want it turned into Cloud Nine.”

I turned it, for the rest of the afternoon.

Chapter 15

Next morning, life went on as before, and yet was entirely different. When I went into the office, they all gave three cheers. Elsie the switchboard girl, the three salesmen, Jack Kefore, Mel Schachtman, and Gordon Carter, and Helen Musick, my secretary, and five minutes later, from the way they acted, you'd have thought I'd always been married—except for Mrs. Musick. She followed me into my private office, wanting to know the "details," especially who the bride was, whether she knew her, and so on. I cut back to the Christmas speech, said I "fell for her then, pretty hard, and began taking her out," then pretended I'd hesitated a bit, on account of the bride-to-be's age, and then "suddenly made up my mind—and that's about all."

At least some of it was true.

I added: "You're coming to dinner tonight."

"Oh no! She doesn't have to do that!"

"She'll be calling you."

"Well I certainly look forward to meeting her!"

Then I got to the things that were waiting for me, mainly

interviews with people who'd called in in response to our Sunday ad, about houses they wanted to list with us, to sell. It was something I couldn't wish off on a salesman, for two reasons: It involves appraisal, which salesmen weren't too good at, and it also involves a risk, the risk of losing a listing, in case the owner wouldn't accept the price I put on his place. In that case, I won't take the property on. I think I've said I lose three out of ten listings that way, but the ones I do get sell fast. But a salesman won't take that responsibility of losing a listing for me, so the result, if you leave it to him, is a bunch of places that hang fire for months, because of some silly price the owner thinks he can get if he just gets tough and holds out for it – while the overhead goes on, the woman who shows it gets sore, and your reputation sags, with the "For Sale" sign out on the lawn for months, where SOLD, *Graham Kirby* is the one thing that builds you up.

So, with a half dozen people waiting, I had to dust out and talk. For the next day I did, and landed four of the six. One of those I landed was typical, a retired admiral, employed by a defense contractor, a helicopter concern, as lobbyist, but now ordered out to San Diego. Of course, he had to get rid of his house, which was in Riverdale, not far from Mother. I called on him Tuesday morning, had a look around, then went inside and told him: "I can sell this place for you."

"The price will be eighty thousand dollars."

He got it off in a rough, quarter-deck voice, not even asking me to sit down. ". . . Wait a minute," I said, choking back a rise in temper. "Who said what the price will be?"

"Well I do, I hope."

"No. You don't, and I don't."

His wife, a quiet little woman in her fifties, looked up at that, and began staring at me. I went on: "Admiral, the buyer will. But it's my business to know what he'll pay, so I'll say what we'll ask. You don't have to take my word –

put your appraiser on it, and if his figure's higher than mine, then I'll stand corrected, and accept what he says. But I'm an appraiser, myself, and I'll be greatly surprised if his figure and mine differ much. But this much I guarantee: You cannot get eighty thousand, and if you insist on that price, you'll wait and wait and wait, and show the place and show it and show it, and lose the interest on your money, which is compounded the first of next month, and pay and pay and pay, for upkeep, water, and taxes—and in the end, you'll have to take seventy thousand, which was all it was worth in the first place."

"The price will be eighty thousand."

"Then get another broker."

I turned to go, but the wife darted in front of me, to block my way to the hall. "Please, Mr. Kirby," she begged me, "don't go—not yet." And then, to him: "Who knows what this place will bring? Mr. Kirby, whose business is real estate, or you, whose business is chopper blades? And who's going to sit here month after month, in Maryland, all alone, while you're in California, living the life of Riley? *I won't have it!* You can't order people to pay eighty thousand dollars, as though they were seamen or something. You can't——"

"The price will be seventy thousand dollars."

I must have glanced at one of the chairs, because he suddenly pushed it toward me and asked me to please sit down. I bowed, thanked him, but waited until she sat down. She did, smiling at me. He sat down and we started to talk, he suddenly uncorking such matters as only an Annapolis man has.

When I got back to the office, Mother was waiting, with a dispatch case full of old pictures of me, "which I thought Sonya might like to have—perhaps for framing." So we sat there a few minutes, going through those old snapshots of me, with the Cabin John grammar school baseball team, with the Northwestern High football team, as a Boy Scout, at the wheel of my first car, and with the gloves on, as a member of the Yale boxing team. And then, suddenly, what she'd really come about: "Gramie, are you asking me to lunch?"

". . . Yes, of course."

"Don't worry, I'll ask permission."

She had Elsie ring Sonya, and then: "Sonya, your mother-in-law." And after the greetings: "I'm here in your husband's office, with some pictures I came across, that I thought you might like to have—and he's asked me to lunch. Is it all right with you if I go? . . . Oh, thank you."

And then when she'd hung up: "You can't do things behind her back—it's protocol. It's the linchpin of marriage."

So we went to the Royal Arms and ordered, and then she drew a long breath. I said: "Cool it—Jane's not a complete fool, and——"

"Gramie, all women are fools. Complete fools."

"She hasn't yet turned into a she-wolf."

"Don't worry, she will."

"And even she-wolves have to eat."

"With you, she might go on a hunger strike."

"Not with the bill collector. And she might, she just very well might, listen to what he says."

"You mean she's beholden to you?"

"She eats when I send the check."

"*Unless* she decides to sell out."

"In which case, we can bid the place in and get started, instead of waiting ten years. Or twenty. Or thirty. These spry, pretty women live a long time. Look at Grandma Moses."

"Then, very well, we'll see."

"So why don't we change the subject."

"Why don't we? Perhaps, at last, I could bring up

what I wanted to talk about. What I had in mind when I fished my invitation."

"I'm sorry—I thought it was Jane."

But, as usual with her when something is really bugging her, she circles around it and past it and by it quite a few times, before zeroing in and getting at what she meant. But then at last: "Gramie, I've been up against it, directly for at least ten years, indirectly longer than that, this problem of men who like women—or we'll say, of a boy who likes them too much. Strangely, not much has been written about them, at least by the psychiatrists. I suppose the reason is the underlying premise of psychiatry, of modern psychiatry, at least, is that sex frustration underlies most mental disorder—in which case these tomcats could seem to be wholly normal, perhaps the only normal people we have. Well, all I can say is, they don't look normal to *me*. And I had the bright idea of hearing what *they* had to say, especially one of them, Casanova, who I got interested in through my weakness for music—I long ago realized that he was the real Don Giovanni, the model for the librettist of that opera——"

She named the librettist, but I don't remember the name. Then she went on: "Casanova was probably the greatest tomcat who ever lived——"

"In college, in one of our courses, the professor called him the greatest literary figure of the eighteenth century."

"I think we could call him that—certainly he was the parent of Dumas, of Hugo, and especially, of Thackeray. But Gramie, by his own revelation, he had a screw loose somewhere. Let me explain what I mean. In Spain he had a rough time, largely through the intrigues of a woman who loused him up, had him thrown into prison, tortured, in all ways treated horribly, and Casanova is most bitter against her, on moral grounds, believe it or not—it seemed she was the daughter of her grandfather, that is, that grandpappy had a few with his own daughter, and this woman was the result. I was quite persuaded myself, and pleased with Casanova that he should see the genetic principle involved. But now watch what happens. He escaped from Spain, of course, and some time later, when he's back in Italy, he runs into a girl, a young married woman, who wants a child and is barren. Gladly, Casanova steps into the breach, or we could say, climbs into the bed. But he knows all the time that this girl is his own daughter. In other words, he commits the very same incestuous offense he complained so bitterly about in Spain. That's what I mean, when I say there was a loose screw, somewhere inside Casanova."

She stopped, ate her lunch for a while, but then went on, right where she left off. "And take Aaron Burr, a real tomcat, who slept up with every boulevard floozie he met on the streets of Paris. Or take Daniel Sickles, perhaps our greatest American tomcat. He married a girl, a complete ninny, and then paid no more attention to her than as though she didn't exist—and he, by the way, was a pupil, in his youth, of—" she named the librettist again, and I still don't remember it— "when he was on the faculty of Columbia College. So Mrs. Sickles had an affair with Barton Key, son of the Key who wrote *The Star-Spangled Banner,* on September 12, 1814—later the birthday of Graham Kirby, a real date in American history—and then Sickles shot Barton Key, shot him and killed him in Lafayette Park, Washington, D.C. He was acquitted, but then, and only then, did he begin to take an interest in this poor, weeping nitwit, who of course had been crucified, this wife, whom he now took back and began sleeping with. It was too much, and shortly after she died—but what kind of depraved nature was it, that felt this unnatural compulsion, to defile her as he did? I tell you, there's a screw loose in these men!"

I may have said something, but don't now recall what it was, and pretty soon she went on: "He was in last night,

Burl I'm talking about, to bring back my trunk and pick up things he'd forgotten. And I told him everything—about the marriage, and also about the miscarriage, as a way of letting him know how completely detached he was, from that girl, for the rest of her life. He just laughed at the idea that she could have miscarried. 'Oh boy,' he crowed, 'there's one for the book—Big Brother decides to marry her, and right away she miscarries.' Then he persuaded himself you're a fag, as he called you, unable to husband Sonya, and for that reason under the necessity of finding a way to pretend that the child she'll have is yours. So you put out this false story, as a way of wiping the slate clean to make way for a new beginning. But then, like Sickles, he gets a pious notion of what he owes this girl and what he owes his child: This 'child of my loins,' as he called it—a regular baptism of his father's semen, so he'll grow up healthy and normal. Gramie, now at last I get to it, what I came to tell you: You must keep her from this madman. She mustn't see him, let him in, or have anything whatever to do with him. Do you hear me, Gramie?"

"I do, but so happens I think I can help."

"What do you mean, help?"

"Cure him of his obsession."

"And how are you going to do that?"

"A good sock on the jaw may help."

"I'd love to see it happen, but I wouldn't."

"Why wouldn't you?"

"Let's get back to Casanova: In London he fell for a girl who played him for a sucker. Who took him for money, and then wouldn't, as they say, put out. He all but lost his mind, it was the turning point of his life. Until then he'd been well-heeled, elegant, and big. After the interlude with her, or without her, actually, he became seedy, necessitous, and petty. I doubt if socking Burl would cure him of his obsession with Sonya, but letting it die of attrition, of not seeing her, of his incorrigible habit of getting somebody else—that might help."

"Okay then we'll freeze him out."

"Gramie, she mustn't see him."

"Well, why would she?"

"She mustn't let him into the house!"

"Well, she knows that, of course!"

"He might invent some trick to get in."

"Will you stop imagining stuff?"

"She mustn't go to this place he's moved into. He's taken over his father's old office, in the Harrison Stuart Building. He's staying there temporarily— "

"I'd call that office a pad."

"Whatever it is, he's living there."

"The pretended private office was all fixed up as a bedroom with bath attached, where your lately deceased husband took lady visitors, mostly women on relief— "

"I know what my late husband did!"

"Then tell it like it was."

She blew her top, and took a moment to calm down again, touching her lips with her handkerchief, and not for some time becoming herself again. I felt more or less like hell, but discussing Harrison Stuart in an easy, quiet way was something I was incapable of. After a while she said: "I'm trying to say she must never go there."

"Okay, you said it."

That afternoon, I talked with more prospects, and one of them kept me until six, so when I got home Helen Musick was there, and Sonya had fixed dinner. It was kind of a funny job, a mixture of Domestic Science, *Joy of Cooking,* and *Mixology,* a pamphlet I had, for drinks. She didn't drink herself, but had put out martini makings, according to the pamphlet—gin, vermouth, lemon peel, and ice, big rocks that she chopped with an icepick, from lumps she froze in cartons. The icepick she put in a table drawer, by the door that led to the rear part of the house, "to remind me," whatever that meant. I made a martini for Helen and me and poured a Coke for her, and we visited, very friendly, with Helen warming to her. Then we had dinner: fruit cup, of melon, grapefruit, and strawberries; roast chicken, peas, new potatoes, and salad, and brick ice cream with brandied cherries. We went back in the living room for more conversation, but around ten Helen left, I taking her out to her car. "I just love her," she whispered. "So natural, so sweet, so friendly—she's *just* the person for you."

"What she have to say?"

"Helen? Well, you heard her."

"Your mother! What did she want?"

"She told you: She brought pictures of me."

"Where are they?"

"At the office—I haven't been there since lunch. I came direct from a guy who wants me to sell his house."

"What did she say? About *her!* Mrs. Sibert?"

"Nothing. I did but she didn't."

"And what did you say?"

"The same, no more, no less."

"Then what did she talk about?"

"Burl, and the torch he's carrying for you. She says you mustn't see him. Mustn't let him in this house, mustn't go to that pad where he lives."

"Does she think I'm a kook or something?"

"I don't know what she thinks, only what she said."

"Burl's not what I'm afraid of."

"Well, I'm not, so that makes two of us."

"Mrs. Sibert *is.*"

"Maybe, but I know nothing to do about it."

"The thing of it is, what *I* do about it."

"For *now,* may I suggest?"

". . . Suggest *what?*"

"Get a cloudy look in your eye."
"Is that all you ever think about?"
"You know something better to think about – ?"
". . . There *isn't* innything better!"
"Peel."
"Carry me upstairs first."
"I'm getting hooked on you. Could it be love?"
"I don't but it's *sump'm.*"

Chapter 16

Then, for three or four weeks, came the period of readjustment, when all kinds of things got done, and we shook down to a new life. Mr. and Mrs. Lang came over, and we straightened the announcements out—they sent envelopes to the office, and I addressed them myself, so they'd be ready when the engraved cards came from the stationer. Then I took Sonya to the bank, to open a personal account. I wanted her added to my account, to make a joint thing of it, but she wouldn't hear of the idea. "I might make some silly mistake," she said, "that would cost you all kinds of money. So she opened her own account, with a check for $1,000 that I gave her, and that covered that. Then there was her car, as well as her driver's license. I got her a little blue Valiant, that she picked out for herself, and sent her to driving school, where she learned fast, and got her license in a couple of weeks.

Then at last she met Modesta, my cleaning woman, and wanted to fire her, but I balked. I said, "So maybe she's not much of a cleaning woman, but what cleaning woman is? There could come a time when you need her bad, so she stays."

Then came the piano, a beautiful little Steinway, a baby grand, and when Sonya saw it she cried. But when she sat down and played, I wanted to cry. I mean, her playing had something, and I saw why Mother had liked it.

And in between, every few nights, she gave little dinners – for Mother, for her parents, for my friends, by twos and fours and sixes, each better than the last, and all of them together kind of easing off the necessity for some kind of general reception. The drinks kept baffling her, and she would peep at her icepick, there in the table drawer, and perhaps it was how she put it in there with the napkins, but it seemed to be some kind of reminder of what she mustn't forget, in the way of bitters, cherries, oranges, or vermouth – none of which did she understand.

And then one afternoon at the office, when I'd just got back from lunch, my phone gave two or three rings I sensed as urgent rings, and when I answered Elsie said: "Mr. Kirby, Mrs. Kirby just called in and said get home at once, *quick!*"

I got there quick, I'm telling you.

When I saw Burl's car outside, you may be sure I didn't waste time on neat, fancy parking. I banged the curb as I banged it, jumped out, went up the front walk at a trot, and stabbed my key in the lock. I was almost afraid to look when I went in the door, but when I did I saw her at once, on one of the living room sofas, a sulky look on her face. On the cocktail table was a tray, with Scotch, ice, and fizz water on it, and off by itself, a half-full highball glass. Burl was at one of the windows beside the fireplace, looking out, and he turned around quick to face me. I hadn't seen him in quite some time, but he hadn't changed much. He was a tall, slim guy, as I've heard Don Juan was, but there was something rawboned about him, as though plenty of strength was there. He had dark eyes like Mother's, and a fairly handsome face. It was nicely chiseled, with kind of a curl to the lip, but what caught your eye about it was its color. He had two red spots on his cheeks that gave him an arrogant, hungry look, and when his big brown eyes opened wide there was something almost animal about it, I mean a predator. Don't get the idea he was just a jerk. Three parts of a somebody were there, and that kept making you wonder why he didn't add up to more. Then for a flash something else would show that was just crafty, or crooked, or mean, or something—not in harmony with the eyes, the mouth, or the color. He greeted me, "Oh, hello," very sour, and then snarled at her: "So that's why you got me a drink—so you could go to the kitchen and put in a call for this crumb?"

"You didn't think I'd *really* give you a drink?" she snapped at him, "unless a glass of warm piss in the face."

"That'll do," I warned her. "*I'm* here."

"Okay, but I wouldn't."

I asked him: "What are you doing here?"

"Why," he answered, "calling on Sonya, of course."

I asked her: "And why did you let him in?"

"Because," she answered, speaking very slow and distinct, "I knew when he'd spoken his piece, through the pigeonhole, that we'd come to a certain point, where things had to be said, so we could make a fresh start, and then life could go on. So I asked him in and put in my call to you. So now we commence with the saying. Go on," she told Burl. "Explain to your brother, please, why you're calling on me."

He glowered, took a seat, and picked up his glass.

"Put that down," she snapped.

He did, and she carried it to the table against the wall, the one where she kept her icepick. Then, to him: "Get going. Tell him."

He glowered some more, but didn't say anything. She went on, herself: "To begin with, he doesn't believe, or says he doesn't, that I had inny miscarriage. He says that's an invention of yours, on account of your being a fag, unable to do it to me, and figuring a slick way that I could have his childwhile you pretend it's yours. And so, he says the child had rights, like to his father's seminal fluid"—she called it *siminal* fluid—"on his unborn head every day, so he'll grow up strong and healthy, and normal in every respect, from the vitamins that it has. So he came here to do his duty, by the unborn child in me, out of the goodness of his heart—or something."

"If you don't mind I've heard enough."

He got it off in an elegant way, slapped his hands on his knees, and got up. But she moved too, and took position to block him. "You don't leave this room," she snarled, "until I say what has to be said."

"For Christ sake, what else has to be said?"

His elegance was wearing off, so he yelled it, but sat down when I motioned him. She sat down, but not on the sofa, this time. She perched on the cocktail table, to look down on him. "Burl," she went on very softly, "did you think it funny, when we were going together, and I got so shook at how you were grieving for Dale, that I wouldn't go with you to that hideaway you had, your father's old suite of offices, in the Harrison Stuart Building? You want to know why that was? It was because you stink. Because to me you smell like feet, feet that haven't been washed."

On that he flinched as though hit with a whip, and screamed, "What do you mean I stink? You bitch! You—"

He had jumped up, so his face was close to hers, but I pushed him back in his seat. She went on: "That hurts, doesn't it? First to be God's gift to women, and then find out you make her puke."

For some moments, there was just the sound of his

panting, while she looked down at him, cold as a lizard. Then she went on: "Now about Gramie, about him being a fag. . . ."

"Which he is all right. I ran into a guy in Japan who went to Yale with him, and the tales he told, oh brother!"

"The lies he told, I think."

"If that's what you think."

"Burl, your brother's not inny fag, and never has been one. So how do I know he's not? He does it to me in the morning, just before we get up; then again in the afternoon, and then again all night. And why he does, he's encouraged. He's encouraged by me, all the time. On account that he smells so nice. Burl, he smells like a man. So don't you come inny more. Could be I'd let you in, and then throw up on you."

I asked her: "You done?"

"I guess so. Throw him out."

I took him by the arm, gave a yank, and marched him to the front door. In the hall, he picked up a jacket I hadn't seen, a gabardine thing that he'd dropped on the phone table. He started to put it on, but I told him: "You can do that outside." He went out, and on the walk began stabbing his hand into the armhole of the jacket. "Maybe this will help," I told him, and popped a cross to his jaw. He went down and I told him, "Get up!" and aimed a kick at his slats. He got up and I let him have it again. I was set for another kick when a hand touched my arm. She was there. "No, Gramie, no," she whispered, very gently.

And then, to him: *"Git!"*

He scrambled to his feet, and she picked up the jacket and tossed it to him, making a face and saying, "Pee-yoo," as though its smell made her sick. Then she lifted my hand to her mouth and kissed my knuckles. "You shouldn't have," she whispered.

"I was telling him not to come back . . ."

"But I already had."

". . . In a way he'd understand."

"Not that I didn't love it. Did you hit him for me?"

"Who do you think?"

"Then, act like it."

"Encourage me, encourage me."

"Let's run upstairs real quick!"

By then he'd put on his coat and got in his car, on the left side, and wound the right-hand window down. "So brother-o'-mine," he called in kind of a singsong, "you're a big bad two-balled studhorse from down by the Rio Grande – but that's not how Gwenny tells it."

"And who the hell is Gwenny?"

"Gwenn Cary. Remember?"

Gwendolyn Cary was the one who showed houses on Sunday, but I had known her as Lynn. ". . . Yeah? And what about her?" I asked.

"Nothing, except she came every night, every night to this house, hoping for a screw, and not once did she get it. But she finally got your number – the boxing stuff at Yale, all that tough talk with the clients, the act you put on with her, *nothing,* she says, but your way of pretending you're a *he,* when you're just a cocksucking fag!"

I drove at him with my fist.

He ducked and I landed on air. I grabbed and got the coat, then tried to pull him to the window, so I could swing with my other hand. But he was crouched on the seat, next to the window wind-up, and turned it without my seeing him. Suddenly the glass jammed on my arm and I was caught. He saw his chance, lurched back to the wheel, snapped his ignition on, gunned his motor and let in his clutch, all in one motion. But he had to back up, to swing clear of a car ahead, so I was jerked along the curb, and my feet went out from under me. He cut his wheel and shot ahead, but then stopped so his tires screamed. She was in front of his car, one hand on her hip, a thick look on her face. "Wind down that window!" she snapped.

"You think I will? *You think I will?* Out of the way, bitch, or I'm killing you! I'm driving this car right over you, I'm—"

I think he would have, but just then my hand jerked loose and I went staggering to pull her out of the way. She stepped aside and waved him on. He roared past her, like some maniac in a drag race. On one of the lawns, a colored woman was staring—on another, a gardener stood with his hose pointed at us; and in the Lieberman house across the street, I could see a face at the window. But she paid no attention. "Honey," she asked, "are you hurt?"

"Not much. Shook up, is all."

"He's no one to monkey with."

"He's a rat, first, last, and all the time."

"He is, but rats aren't dumb."

She led me inside and up to our bathroom, where she snapped on the light and looked at my hand, which was scratched from the jerk I'd given it to get clear. It bled, too. She got out the Listerine bottle, uncorked it, and bathed my hand with it. "It'll hurt," she said. "It'll sting a little—"

"I can stand it—"

"But then you won't have any infection."

She sprayed bandage on and the bleeding stopped. Then she knelt to my leg, and for the first time I saw my knee, all bloody inside the torn slack. She stripped me down, swabbed more Listerine on, and sprayed me with bandage again. Then she led me into the bedroom, got out my pajamas and started taking my clothes off. "Hey, what are you doing?" I asked.

"You're going to bed, Gramie."

"What for? You think I'm sick or something?"

"You're staying here, I'm bringing your dinner up."

"I have a better idea."

"Yes? What is it?"

"How about *you* peeling off? And coming to bed?"

". . . Who was Gwenn Cary?"

"Well how would I know?"

"Who was she?"

". . . Girl. Woman. Widow. Showed houses for me."

"And came here to get screwed?"

"Ask me no questions I'll tell you no lies."

"Well? Did she?"

"How do I know what she came for?"

"*Did* she?"

"All right, then. She did."

"And you screwed her?"

"Yes, but this was before I met you. It was before my speech at Northwestern, before I ever *saw* you."

"On that bed, on our cloud?"

"But it wasn't a cloud then."

"But on our bed?"

"On one of these beds, I suppose."

I picked up the phone, dialed the store where her mother worked, and asked for "Mrs. Lang, in house furnishings." After some time she came on, and I said: "Mrs. Lang, do you remember those twin beds you sold me, for my master bedroom?" She said she did, and was startled when I asked her to send out duplicates. She kept asking if something was wrong, but I told her: "No, nothing at all, but our woman spilled furniture polish on them, and Sonya can't get out the smell, so. . . ."

So she took over at once, saying new mattresses would take care of that, and I had to argue endlessly that I wanted new beds, the works. At last she agreed, and had me wait while she wrote up the slip. Then: "I'll put an expedite on it," and I was free to hang up. I called Goodwill Industries, and asked them to send for a couple of beds, both in good condition. They said they'd do it next day.

I got out of bed and moved to the room across the hall, turned the bed down and got in. I sang out: "If that takes care of the matter, I'm here waiting for you." She came in, unzipping her dress. Then: "Why would she say that?"

"Why would who say what?"

"This Gwinny, whatever her name was?"

"Husband perhaps. He may have heard stuff. She got married—or at least, so she told me over the phone, I haven't seen her since."

"You mean, if she was seen coming here, she could tell him *that,* and more or less get away with it, that she didn't get screwed by you?"

"Do you *have* to keep using that word?"

"It's the one he used. Is that what you mean?"

"Something like that, could be."

"Is that where *he* got the idea?"

"Burl? That occurred to me too. He had it before he came here, before he said it today. It's what he told my mother, right after we got married."

"You think he believes it?"

"I think he can't bear the idea that you could want somebody else, and at the same time not want him. I think he's diseased on the subject."

"Either way, Gramie, it pees on our cloud. If it was true, it does, and if it wasn't, it does too. But that's Burl all over—he's got a strictly heads-I-win-tails-you-lose mind."

"Do you mind if we talk about something else?"

"I'm talking, he peed on our cloud."

"Not unless you let him. I didn't. *My* cloud is as clean as it was the day we first saw it, down at Ocean City, while we were swimming around. Remember?"

". . . We don't have but one cloud."

"Then let's not let him befoul it. Be-pee it."

At that she seemed to buckle, and yet she closed her zipper. "I have to be going down, if I'm to get you your dinner."

She went, and I lay there some time, in a puddle of pee of my own, that I hadn't mentioned to her. Because from what she had said before, what she had said while he was here, and what she had said just now, it suddenly dawned on me that she knew this guy quite well, much better than I ever knew him, brother or not. That wasn't saying too much, but it also had dawned on me that he knew her pretty well—why it griped me, I don't know, but it did, that he knew and I didn't, that she liked malts with egg, which was something he had shouted about. It meant nothing, and yet it sat sour on my stomach, or left the bed feeling damp, or bugged me, somehow. Then while I was thinking about it, the phone rang and then suddenly stopped, which meant she had taken it, probably in the kitchen. Then her voice floated up: "It's for you."

I trotted to the master bedroom, where the upstairs extension was, and answered. "Gramie!" came a well-remembered voice. "Your kept woman is back!"

"Well Jane!" I stammered. "Welcome! Welcome!"

"When am I going to see you?"

"Ah—soon, I hope."

"Tonight? You taking me to dinner?"

"Well—I'm hooked for tonight, but——"

I talked and talked, trying to say something, while at the same time saying nothing, and pretty soon she cut in: "Who was that girl who answered?"

"Why—my wife. Jane, I got married."

She didn't say anything, even when I spoke her name a few times and asked if she was there. Then I was getting a dial tone, and realized she'd hung up. I hung up, then heard the bell go *clink,* which it did when another extension hung up—meaning it had been open, with Sonya listening in, while the call went on. I went back to the other bedroom, lay down, and tried to think. In a few minutes came the sound of our dinner bell, a tiny thing that tinkled, one of Sonya's little gags. Then there she was at the door, bringing in my tray. She set it on a bench beside the bed, asked: "Would you like me to make the martini?"

"Please."

She made it, raised her glass, said: "Mud in your eye," and took the one sip she would take, to keep me company with it. I said what fine martinis she made. Then: "That was Jane Sibert. You listened in?"

"Well? I had to know if you took the call."

"Then, you know what was said."

"Or wasn't said."

"That's right—she kind of cut it short."

For some time nothing was said. Then I blurted: "Well?"

"Well? *Pop.*"

". . . *Pop?* Is that what you said?"

"Like the weasel. How does a weasel go *pop?*"

"In olden times, a tobacco pouch was a weasel."

"Oh! That explains it. I've wondered about it."

"Well now you know. Where does Jane come in?"

"She did it. Made our cloud go *pop.*"

"Stop trying to be funny."

"I'm not. Our cloud has just gone *pop,* and we're going to go *bump,* as soon as we hit the ground, which could be inny time, now."

"Personally, I don't borrow trouble."

"Personally, I don't have to."

Chapter 17

But nothing happened that day that sounded like *bump,* or like anything.

I ate my dinner and she took the tray. I lay there awhile, and apparently she ate in the kitchen. Then I heard the TV and went down in my robe. We both looked at the news, then at some show, and then went to bed, still in the guest bedroom. I took the bed I'd been in, she the other. I tried to entice her to my bed, but she didn't seem to hear.

In the morning she got up first, and I peeped at her while she dressed. Then I got up and got dressed, went down and had breakfast, which she served me in the dining room. As I was finishing the doorbell rang, and when I opened it there was Mother, looking fairly frazzled.

When I asked what brought her at this ungodly hour, she said: "I wanted to catch you before you left for your office," but instead of saying why, she got off about my hand, which by now showed scabby cuts through the bandage. I told her it got caught in the car door, "so I raked the skin off getting it loose." She didn't go further with it, but let me take her into the living room.

There Sonya joined us, chiming in about my hand: "It's really a mess, but I did what I could with what we had in the medicine chest."

That seemed to be that.

Then: "What did you do to Jane?" Mother asked me.

"I didn't do *anything* to her."

"She was over last night, in a perfectly terrible state."

I told about the phone call, and she said: "She had a complete crack-up, so I had to drive her home and take a taxi back. I tried to get her to stay, but she said she had to be alone, 'to face herself, and what's left of her life.'"

"Mrs. Stu," asked Sonya, "what's it going to mean? That she'll cut Gramie out of her will?"

"I'm afraid so. She's the best friend I have on this earth, but she's rocked to the heels, and I can't quite picture her leaving things as they are."

"You mean on account of me?"

"You said it, Sonya. But since you ask me, yes."

"I can't quite picture it either."

"I can't quite picture her starving for love."

I got it off pretty sour, as it seemed to me that Sonya, last night, and now Mother today, had jumped to hasty conclusions, by taking stuff for granted that might or might not happen. "Cracked up or down or sidewise, she still has to eat, and she *won't* eat without cashing my check. Likewise, until now, she's been the best friend *I* have on earth—just the same she's going to get hungry. So I'm going to hold everything, wait with my fingers crossed, till my check goes out next week, and see what she does with it. If she cashes it as I expect, then we take it from there, and I rather imagine she'll find there's quite a lot left of her life—once she quits being silly. If not, then we can talk things over."

Neither of them seemed to hear me. Sonya asked: "Mrs. Stu, would you like some coffee?"

"Sonya, I'd love it."

So Sonya made her coffee the way she likes it, with milk—*café au lait,* from freeze-dry coffee, with sugar lumps, in a glass, with a silver coaster she'd bought. Mother stirred it, touched her tongue to the clots of coffee, and asked: "Sonya, was that your arrangement of 'Chopsticks' you played at the school that day?"

Sonya stared, then went over, knelt, put her head on Mother's shoulder, and whispered: "Oh, Mrs. Stu, just to think you *noticed,* that you remember it now, what I played!"

"I loved it," said Mother. "Play it."

So she went to the piano, while Mother moved to the bench beside her, still holding the coffee, and played some crazy arrangement of "Chopsticks." "I just boogie-woogied the left hand," she explained. "But of course, as boogie-woogie's four-four and Chopsticks is six eights, there was kind of an accent problem, till I fudged them together a bit."

"It's most effective," said Mother.

"Will you kindly tell me," I asked, "what 'Chopsticks' *or* boogie-woogie has to do with the price of fish, or Jane Sibert, or her farm, or *anything* we've been talking about?"

"It has plenty to do with it!" screamed Sonya, jumping up. "It means it's not my fault! It means she's not blaming me."

"Well I'm certainly *not* blaming you," said Mother.

"Thanks, Mrs. Stu. Thanks, thanks."

She plumped down on the bench again and started to cry. "Mrs. Stu," she blubbered, "would you do something for me? I know I have to go, I said I would, I promised, that I wouldn't be inny pest, and I won't be. I offered to go before, right here in this very room, the morning we got married, but he said do as he said, or he'd give me a boot in the tail; when he boots me in the tail is when I love him so. So I did. But now everything's changed.

"Mrs. Stu, would you kid her along a little? Tell her hold

everything, that things are going to get better, so wait for the silver lining, so I have a few days to think. To face what's left of *my* life. To figure out what I'm going to do?"

"Put it that way, Sonya, I have to."

"I do put it that way."

"Then I'll do what I can."

At last this queer conversation ended, and Mother left. I left, and carried on business as usual, I don't recall the details. When I got back that night, Goodwill had come for the beds, and Sonya seemed feverishly pleased they were gone, giving the subject no peace.

Late that night Mother called, and when she made sure Sonya was there, on the kitchen extension I mean, she gave her first report: "She was over tonight, and I started in on Sonya's campaign, to kid her along, as she said, and try to persuade her to wait, to keep a stiff upper lip, to look on the bright side, 'until things have a chance to change.' She seemed to feel better, sensing something, under sly hints, and was able to drive home herself."

Sonya seemed pleased, when she joined me in the living room, and I can't quite say that I was, but of course I was playing a different ballgame, one that wouldn't start until my check went out, the first of the following week. If it got cashed, it seemed to me the kidding along would stop, and we could make a fresh start, so life would go on from there. If not, I doubted if kidding along would help, or that anything would.

The next day, the next night, were practically a retake, but the night after that was different, I'm here to tell you it was. Mother called late, as usual, around midnight I would say, and from the very first word she spoke, acted all wrung up and excited. She wouldn't begin until she made sure that Sonya was on the extension and could hear what she would say.

"Chillens, hold your breath and hold on to your hats...it worked, Sonya's idea did, beyond our wildest dreams, her dreams, my dreams, and Gramie's dreams, all of our dreams, put together. Feature this if you can: She's resigned to losing Gramie—she loves him, that she betrays with every word she says, but knows she can't get him back. But, she's leaving the farm to *me!* To *me*—or in other words, the dream is left as it was, because on this, of course, Gramie and I are one! She's leaving it all to me, and all because Sonya made me kid her along. Made me act with compassion, made me do the decent thing by a stricken soul, because she was willing to do the decent thing! I'm so happy I could sing."

"Mrs. Stu," yelped Sonya, "how *wonderful!*"

"Sonya, you don't *have* to go!"

"Well not that I ever *wanted* to!"

It went on for at least twenty minutes, with Mother giving details of how Jane "had thought it over all day, and then was ready, when she came, to say what she would do"; and also giving credit to Sonya, for thinking the idea up of smoothing Jane down and stringing it out, and heading the explosion off. And then at last when she hung up, came the sound of running feet, and the clutch of arms flung around me. I carried her up to our cloud, and we stayed on it all night, all next day, which was Sunday, and all Sunday night.

Or part of Sunday night.

Sunday evening, being exact.

The phone rang around twelve, and we both went piling downstairs, but I didn't lift the receiver, there on the hall phone, until she gave me a shout from the kitchen. Then I answered, but all I could hear at the other end was what sounded like somebody crying. I said: "Hello? Hello? *Hello?*" but still nothing was said.

Then Sonya asked: "Mrs. Stu, is that you?"

"Yes, Sonya. . . . I'm sorry."

"Where are you? Home?"

"Yes. In bed."

"But what happened?"

"Sonya, everything happened. She came over again, and was friendlier than ever—she'd called Mort Leonard, her lawyer, and made arrangements to see him tomorrow. And so on and so on. And then *he* had to come!"

"He? Who's he?"

"Well who do you think?"

"Burl?"

"He walked from that dump he has to bring back a corkscrew he took, by mistake, thinking I might need it. That's all it took."

"You mean, he told how Gramic beat him up? Or what?"

"He told about your pregnancy!"

"Well that was nice of him!"

"I hadn't mentioned it to her; well why should I? It was no business of hers! But she turned on me like a viper for 'concealing the truth from her!'. . . don't ask me to tell you the rest. He treated her like his child, patting her, kissing her, calming her. Perhaps women are his specialty, and perhaps I don't respect it, but don't think he's not good at it, that he doesn't know how to handle them. They left together—as soon as she could talk, she offered to drive him home. That was a half hour ago—I called as soon as I could. Now *I've* been like something demented."

"Mrs. Stu, don't take it so hard."

She came, when Mother hung up, but not on running feet, and we went upstairs very slow, taking separate beds once more. I turned out the light, and after a long time she turned it on.

"Her check goes out tomorrow? Is that what you said, Gramie?"

"It's due out tomorrow, yes."
"If I were you, I'd take it in person."
"And have it out with her? Why?"
"At least you'll know where you stand."

Chapter 18

So I went over there, around 9:30 the next morning, first stopping by the office, where Helen Musick drew the check, and when I'd signed it, put it in an envelope for me, marked "Mrs. Sibert." I parked out front, went up on the porch, and rang.

Almost at once came her voice: "Who is it?"

Thinking fast I decided to stall, because if I said my name, she might decide not to come to the door, and just leave me standing there. So, raising my voice to change it, I called: "Special Delivery!"

She answered: "Just a moment, please," and I heard movement inside. Then the chain bolt rattled and she opened the door, but when she saw who it was, tried to close it. But I was ready for that, and shoved my foot inside the jamb, so she couldn't. She tried to kick my shin, but had on tennis shoes, and hurt herself, so she winced. But it took long enough for me to take note of her changed appearance.

She had on a blue gingham dress I'd seen a hundred times, white socks, and the white sneakers. Her top two buttons were open, to show quite a bit of cleavage, and her hair had a ribbon on it, a new frill for her. And if it was the ribbon, the buttons, or what, I can't rightly say, but there was something gamy about her that wasn't like her at all.

After a moment she snapped: "What are you doing here at this hour? Pretending to be the postman?"

I told her, "I said 'Special Delivery' and very special it is—I brought you your check."

"Then, I'll take it."

"You will when you've asked me in."

"Very well. But give me a moment, please."

She disappeared, and I heard her going upstairs. Then she was back, holding the door wide, and I went into a place I knew like the palm of my hand, and yet never got used to. I mean, it was more like a gag, a museum someone thought up, a stage set to play a comedy in, than a sure-enough, actual house.

In the hall was a cozy-corner, in under the turn of the stairs, consisting of built-in seat, with Navajo blanket on it, and leather cushions with Indian heads burned on. Over the seat were pipe racks, and over the pipes, college pennants, mostly M.A.C., for Maryland Agricultural College, which was what the university was called before they bigged it up. Facing the stairs was a hat rack, and on the floor was a hooked rug. There wasn't any living room, of the kind a modern house had, but instead there was a "parlor," and beyond that a "library." In the parlor were horsehair sofas, marbletop tables, wax flowers under glass, vases of gilded cattails, a bookcase with a ship model on it, and steel engravings of the Three Graces, Paolo and Francesca, and Grover Cleveland. On the floor was an Axminster rug, and in a corner a square piano. Everything was just as it had been, except for the smell of bacon frying, which had a meaning, as I realized later, though when I first went in I paid no attention to it.

She led me into the parlor, drew herself up, and said: "You may sit down if you wish."

"Well I damn well wish."

"Don't you dare swear at me!"

"Hey, hey, hey, come off it, this is me—and anything short of poking you one in the jaw comes under the head of gentle, considerate kindness. What was the big idea, hanging up on me?"

"What was the big idea, playing that trick on me?"

"And what trick did I play on you?"

She had left me an opening, I thought, and I was ready to let her have it at one word about my marriage. But she crossed me up. Pointing to a chair and waiting until I took it, she came over, looked down at me, and whispered: "Leading me on as you did! Play acting at being a man, and all the time not being one. Being nothing but a vegetable in human form!"

"You mean, like a potato?"

"More like an onion, slippery inside."

"How does an onion lead a girl on?"

"With all those flowers and music and wine."

"Thought you *liked* flowers and music and wine."

"Oh I do, any woman does. *But* for what they pledge, not for what they are. And in your case, they were just a false front, a way of imitating masculinity while lacking the thing itself."

"You sure?"

"Well I certainly am *now!*"

"Now? What's now?"

"Since the truth was revealed unto me."

"Yeah? By whom?"

Of course, by now I knew by whom, but wanted to make her name him. However, once more she crossed me up.

"By you!" she quavered, almost in tears. "Oh you made it plain, that I have to say—with no beating around the bush, in any way, shape or form. 'Jane, I got married'—if that didn't say it, it can't be said in words."

"That I'm an onion."

"If not, why did you marry this girl?"

"I wanted to—that's why."

"You had to! She's pregnant by your brother!"

"*Was* pregnant by my brother."

"She still is! What kind of cock-and-bull story was that? You take her to the beach, and—lo and behold—she aborts. Could anyone, any grown-up, adult person, actually believe that?"

"God could—He did it."

"Ah, God. *God!*" And then: "You should be asking for God's forgiveness, that you would pretend He's responsible. Of course, I find it in me, even so, to pity this poor girl, the life you've invited her to—having all a woman's desires, and none of her satisfactions."

"She gets satisfied every night."

"*I* never got satisfied!"

"You know why?"

"Tell me why!"

My mouth was primed to let her have it, to tell her she was too old for such satisfactions, at least as supplied by me, but somehow the words didn't come. I heard myself say, in a moment, "You're so beautiful I didn't have the heart."

Her answer to that was to sneer, and then, sitting primly on the edge of a chair, she proceeded to tell me off, speaking slow and going into details—how my whole life had been a pretense of being something which I was not, of desperate playacting, with my athletic career at Yale, my jumping my arm muscles up, when we'd go swimming at Chesapeake Beach, my picking brawls with people, "though sometimes you meet your match." She pointed to my hand, which was still scabbed up, and went on and on and on. It was all part of the same old record I'd heard a few times before, so it was no trouble to know where it came from, or why it appealed to her: It put a totally different light on those years of not being passed-at by me.

So sometimes my attention wandered, and I had a chance to think. One of those times I woke up to the bacon smell in the air, and the thing of it was what I hadn't remembered before: She didn't like bacon, so who'd she been cooking it for? Why did she duck upstairs before bringing me in?

"Okay," I said, "if that's how I prove masculinity, what are we waiting for? Why not prove it here and now, by beating you up, Mrs. Sibert? You have a pretty cute backside—come on, I'll blister it for you!" With that I grabbed her hand and yanked her out of her chair. *"No!"* she screamed. *"No! No! No!"*

Vloomp, vloomp, vloomp!

When I looked he was on the stairs, piling down fast, a hammer in his hand, one she kept on her dressing table, don't ask me why. "Why!" I said. "Duh! I thought that would smoke you out!"

"Gramie, leave her alone."

"Hand me the hammer or I'm taking it off you."

He was still in the hall, and I marched myself out there, slow. Now there's something about a big guy, walking toward you step by step, that somewhat dampens courage, and that's how it was with him. I held out my hand and he gave me the hammer, handle first, though giving the head a flip to indicate his contempt. I motioned him into the parlor. "Sit down," I said. "The both of you, sit down."

They sat, and I asked him: "You spent the night in this house?"

"What's it to you where I spent the night?"

"Answer me!"

"Yes!" she whined. "With me! In my bed!"

"Having intimacies with you?"

"Oh! And how! More than *you* ever did!"

"It would appear I've been missing something."

"It certainly would, Mr. Graham!"

"Okay, let's get on."

"Let's not! You may give me my check and go!"

"Honey, you're not taking his check."

He went over, knelt by her chair, put his arms around her, and kissed her. She inhaled him, and it crossed my mind, he may have smelled like feet to Sonya, but apparently smelled different to her.

She kissed him, and said, "When I take money off a crumb, I figure he's still a crumb, but I've got the money."

"But Honey, *I* have money."

"Oh Burl, my little Burl—that's the sweetest thing that ever was said to me, that ever was said to me in my whole life."

"The reason is, I love you."

"Now you're making me cry."

She mumbled kisses all over his cheek, and then he turned to me. "So, brother-o'-mine, we're done. Beat it."

"Just a moment," she said.

"You taking this check or not."

"I've been forbidden to take it, so *no*. But there's one more thing, Gramie. Did you bring my will too?"

"Your will's at the bank, in my box."

"I want it. I want it today."

"You'll get it, when I find it convenient to open my box at the bank, get it out, and bring it to you."

"Mail it over, you mean."

"I'll say what I mean, Mrs. Sibert."

"I want my will!"

"I bid you good day."

"And a good day to you, Gramie, boy—and it is a good day for you, come to think if it, isn't it? Here I get the girl with the looks and the shape and the million-dollar farm, but look what you get, Gramie. The girl with the bastard inside—and my little bastard at that, which guarantees he's really good stock. You lucky dog!"

"How'd you like to go to hell?"

"If this be hell, they ought to charge me for it!"

As I left, she burst into silvery laughter.

I went home to make my report, and found Mother waiting for me, with Sonya, over *café au lait* in the living room. They both listened, and all Sonya said was: "At least you know where you stand."

"Poor thing, she's not old—Jane is fifty-eight, still in rosy middle age, and she was forty-three when she took you, Gramie, widowed, wet, and willing. So you let her down—I'm still amazed at that, as I had taken for granted, all this time ever since, that she had an arrangement with you. But if that's how it was, that's how it was.

"Anyway, for fifteen years she yearns and nothing happens. And then one day, you jolt her back teeth out by calmly announcing, 'Jane, I got married.' That she can't forgive you. And then, to top it off, appears this practiced seducer, and the rest was a foregone conclusion. But it *had* to come sooner or later, once you and Sonya got married. That it came with Burl was unfortunate, but it's her life, and we can't choose for her. Still, I should call Stan Modell."

Stan Modell was our lawyer, and she called from the hall extension, with me standing by, in case. The call went on for some time, after she sketched out what had happened, touching on Burl lightly, and bearing down on the will. When she hung up she said, "He wants to see me this afternoon, wants me to come to his office, so he can look things up, in connection with her farm, and 'try to work something out,' as he said. But he says hang on to the will—under no circumstances let it out of your hands.

We don't know what will come up, and if you have it you have it."

So it seemed I'd done the right thing, in giving Jane a stall about sending it back. Sonya suggested that Mother come to the house, when she got back from Upper Marlboro, "so I can give you dinner, and you won't do any talking at Gramie's office about it." Mother agreed and accepted, and left.

I left, for a day that was endless—I had two houses to look at, to get the history of, to make an appraisal on, and it took me all afternoon, until after six o'clock. But at that I got home before Mother, who had had to wait in Stan's office until Mort Leonard got back from a trip to the District and could talk when Stan called him.

"I heard the call," said Mother. "Stan made it perfectly plain that he felt we had a suit, the basis for an action, to recover the money you've paid, the ten thousand or so Jane's accepted, in return for the will she drew, making you her beneficiary. But he wasn't exactly threatening—he was 'hoping it wouldn't be necessary,' and reminding Mort of what it might mean to Jane to have it come out in a lawsuit that though she pretended to farm this land, she was actually living off you, so the farm was not her main income, and her *Rural Agricultural* tax status more or less, mostly more, phony. These lawyers can figure angles, but I told him hold his horses, not to move unless I gave the word.

"Gramie, I don't know much, but this much I've learned in my life: Stay out of lawsuits. It looks as though we've lost it, *but* if we just do nothing, refrain from aggravation, and mark time, Jane *may* come to her senses, *may* kick this scavenger out, *may* resume her life. After all, she's not married yet."

"I'm sorry to say she is."

That was Sonya, very quiet. She'd brought the cocktail

tray, and was watching me stir the martinis. "What did you say?" I asked her.

"She got married. To Burl."

"She couldn't. In Maryland, they must wait two days, as who knows better than we do, before they can get their license."

"They drove to Dover, Delaware, and had it done there. She called from the motel they're in—she wanted you to know, 'wanted Gramie to be the first one.' Also she asked me to tell you, don't bother about the will, sending it back to her. She's having a new one drawn when she gets back tomorrow, leaving the farm to Burl, and voiding the one you have."

I poured the martini, raised my glass, said "Mud in your eye." But Mother didn't raise hers, and Sonya didn't raise hers, and pretty soon Mother said: "I'm scrubbing her—putting her out of my mind."

"Well I certainly am," I assured her.

"You're not, Mrs. Stu isn't, and I'm not."

Mother stiffened so you could see it, not being used to that kind of talk, from a sixteen-year-old snip. But Sonya went right on: "Father was here when she called, and the first thing he said was: 'Jesus, who's on that hook now?'"

"He has that hook on the brain."

I was fairly disagreeable about it, but she kept her cool as she said: "Yes, he has, hasn't he? It rides him all the time."

But Mother cut in then, very cold, and very much in the grand style: "Sonya, I'm done with Mrs. Sibert, so stop talking about her please, as I've heard all I mean to listen to on a most unpleasant subject."

"Mrs. Stuart, I think you mean."

"Ah yes, Mrs. Stuart, of course."

"Your daughter-in-law has the same name as you."

"Sonya, I've accepted your correction."

"And in my house, I decide what I talk about."

"Very well, I withdraw my remark."

"And you're listening, whether you mean to or not."

If Mother replied to that, I don't just now recollect, but Sonya had cut her to size, and now got up from her chair and sashayed over to her, in kind of a slow way she had, one hand on her hip. "So the dream," she said, "is kerflooie—the white moon, the white shells, the white cotton, are gone, *except the lilies aren't*."

"When did lilies get in it?" I snapped.

"White ones, on Miss Jane, before they close the lid."

"Of the coffin, you mean?"

"The casket, they call it now."

That settled my hash for a while, as it was the part of the dream I tried not to think about.

She went on then, to Mother: "You're not scrubbing Miss Jane—she's married to your son." Then, to me: "And you're not—she's been your godmother, and she's now your brother's wife." And then, tapping her own wishbone: "And I'm not—I'm the cause of it all." And after letting that much sink in: "One of us, one of us three in this room, is on that hook, the one my father worries about. Because, if she signs a new will, making Burl her heir, she won't live to see the snow—it'll drift down on her grave before it falls on her. Somebody here must see that she doesn't die."

She picked up her cocktail glass, raised it, and said: "Here's to the lucky one, whichever of us gets elected."

Chapter 19

Hook or no hook, the summer dragged on, and what had been a beautiful dream, with us up there on our cloud, had turned into an ugly nightmare, but not one that you hoped would end, because somehow you knew the awakening was going to be still worse. I carried on, I got listings. I helped the salesmen, I closed deals, though it was all tougher than usual, as the recession was on, and things were slow, terribly slow.

But all that time the other was bugging me, especially Stan Modell. Couple of days after that evening with Mother, he called with news of the new will, which he'd got from Mort Leonard—Jane had drawn it, making Burl her heir, had it witnessed, signed it, and handed it over to him. Stan was all hot to sue, to recover the ten thousand I'd paid, "or at least draw the papers, and out of courtesy show them to Mort. Graham, he dare not let that suit come to trial. Because if it comes out in court, that while claiming to farm her land, to enjoy Rural Agricultural assessment, she was actually deriving her main income from you, that does it. They pop her up to her proper status, on the basis of actual value, *probably retroactive,* so she'll be eaten alive by taxes. She'll have to do something about you, at the very least refund your ten thousand dollars. It's not hay, Graham—and what do you have to lose?—I'll carry the load, on a contingent basis, of course, and all *you* have to do is nothing."

I told him I'd think about it.

I told him on Mother's phone, where I did all my talking with him, on call-backs I'd give him, when he'd ring me at the office. He'd call, I'd tell him stand by, and then go running out and drive to Mother's. Helen Musick thought I'd gone nuts, and who am I to say I hadn't? Of course, when I'd hang up on a call, I'd talk it out with Mother, who was still dead set against suing.

"Gramie," she told me very solemn, "you'll do as you like, of course, and Stan's idea sounds good—certainly she has her nerve, to be keeping the money you've paid her. Just the same, who says you'll get it back? Suppose the court holds that while you were paying her, you were actually heir to her land, if she had died in that time, and would have inherited. When she didn't die, you had assumed a risk and lost, on the principle of insurance, and have no refund coming.

"Also, Gramie, suppose she says, suppose she swears in open court, after coaching from we-know-who, that wedlock was part of the deal, that you promised to marry her, after spending years in her bed, but when out of the blue, you up and married a young girl, she decided to call it off. Don't forget, you lived for ten years in her house, and the bed may be hard to disprove.

"I'm against the lawsuit, Gramie. It would be wonderful, I'd love it myself, I confess, to get a judgment against her that Burl would have to pay, out of that money he made, from poor little Dale Morgan's death—but it might not turn out that way, and I'd simply hate it, his laughing at us in court, the wolfish grin he'd give it, in case we lost, which we might very well do. It's a wrench to give up that dream, it had become part of me. But let's face it, it's gone! It's not there any more! Well, life is like that! I say let's forget it!"

"Amen, I say it too!"

". . . We can't forget it!"

She screamed at me, after one of Stan Modell's calls, marching up and down, digging her fingernails in, and nipping her lip with her teeth. "We're in one key, the orchestra in another, as your little wife reminded us, that evening at your house. *Jane won't live to see the snow,* that's what we're up against, unless something is done! So she's a nut, a screwball, a kook, but we always knew that, didn't we? Now she's a screwball with a bad egg winding her up, a Trilby who met her Svengali—but can we hold it against her?

"The main thing is, she'll be hit by some horrible accident, as Dale Morgan was hit, and for exactly the same reason—*so he can cash in on it big!* So okay, okay, okay, now we're on key, at last. But what do we do about it? What *can* we do about it? Go to the police? What do we know to tell them? Let Stan Modell file his suit? What good is that going to do? Go to her? Warn her? Then *he* could file suit against *us*. And, it wouldn't do any good, not in her present mood. Can you think of anything, Gramie?"

"Not right now I can't."

"I'm at my wits' end, I confess."

I'd have given anything to talk all that out with Sonya, but something came up, so I couldn't. The beds were delivered, and Modesta made them up, so they looked identically the same as the ones that were taken away. And I got into mine, pleased to be back again in our own proper room.

And I waited and waited and waited, but nobody came in there with me. I called, and she answered, from across the hall in the guest room. I went over there, and she was in bed, in the same bed she'd been sleeping in, reading *Playboy*. I asked if she wasn't coming in with me, and she said: "Better I sleep in here."

At that I blew my top. "In what way better?" I asked. "You keep screeching that you're my wife. Has it occurred to you, I'm your husband? Get out of that bed! Get in there, where you belong!" I ripped the covers off her and tried to pull her out, but she fought me off, stronger than you might think. I wound up slapping her and she started to cry. So a woman in tears calls for love, and God knows I was willing. But these weren't that kind of tears. They came in heaves and twitches and jerks, and had a bitter sound. I tried to ease her, but she wouldn't relax to let me. Then I went back to my room, sobbing worse than she was. So I couldn't talk anything out with her, not in a friendly way.

And then one day, at the office, came a mysterious call, from some guy I probably knew. "Mr. Kirby," he said, "if you'll drive down past the playground, the playground by the creek, where Forty-fourth intersects, you're going to see something, you're going to get a surprise." I paid no attention, but went back to work, for at least eighteen seconds. Then I had Elsie ring the house. When no answer came I went down and got headed for Forty-fourth Avenue.

The "playground" is only a halfway thing, mainly grass and bushes and trees, with a brook running down the middle that's really the head of Anacostia Creek. One or two rustic benches are there, but no restrooms or supervision, so parents don't like it and forbid their kids to go there, with the results it's usually deserted. It was deserted today, as I drove past on Forty-fourth, except for two people, lolling around on the grass, one Burl Stuart, the other Sonya Kirby. I drove by in a hurry, then at East-West stopped and took a U-turn, to go back. When I did I spotted their cars, her Valiant down near the bridge, his Pinto behind it. I drove by once more, slowing down a little to stare, and at Understood pulled in and stopped. I debated whether to go back, to stop and have it out, with her, with him, with both of them, but somehow couldn't. I wish I could say I had some good reason, a deep reason that made sense, but it wouldn't be true. I just lost my nerve, couldn't make myself.

I drove back to the office and sat down at my desk again. Helen Musick came in, had a look at me, and wanted to know the trouble. I told her, "Nothing." But she took me down and drove me around in her car, making me open the wing, so the cool air blew on my face. Then she took me in People's and bought me a Coke. It revived me enough so I was able to carry on, the rest of the afternoon.

At last, around six, I got home and Sonya got up from reading the afternoon paper, the *Evening Star.* She brought me the cocktail tray, but I said: "I don't care for anything."

"Well you may as well have one."

"I said I don't want it!"

"Listen, you don't have to yell."

So we sat there a minute, and then, very casually, she said: "I saw you drive by today. Why didn't you stop?"

"Some particular reason I should have?"

"Well after all it was me."

"And also Burl Stuart."

And then, as sour stuff boiled up in my throat, I went over and bellowed: "Why? Why was he there with you?"

"I said you don't have to yell!"

"Answer me! What was he doing there?"

By that time, I was in slapping range, and might have fired one at her, except that she turned into something I was always forgetting she was, a brash teenager. She snapped a kick at my stomach, which I flinched away from in time, but it shut me up. She sulked a moment, then said, as though talking to a child: "What was he doing there? Well if I told him to meet me there, how could he, without *being* there?"

"*You?* Told him to *meet* you there?"

"That's right. Now you know."

"He called you, he. . ."

"No, no! I called him!"

"*You?* Called *him?* At his home? And. . ."

"Well you seem to know all about it."

"Sonya! I'm asking you!"

"At his office I called him, of course."

"What did you call him about?"

"To 'gradulate him, on his marriage. It was the least I could do, I thought. After all we had been friends."

"And, he raped you—a real friendly thing."

"I try not to think about that."

"I do too, unsuccessfully."

"You needn't make cracks, Gramie."

"Couldn't you *'gradulate* him over the phone?"

"Yes, of course. I did."

"Then why the grass sandwich out in the park?"

"That was his idea. He said come up to his office, he wanted to see me. But I said meet me outside."

"What did he want of you?"

"Screw me, was all."

"I told you to refrain from using that word!"

"Well you asked what he wanted of me!"

"And what did you tell him?"

"Told him no, for the reason he already knew, as I'd told him that day at the house. So he said I should reconsider, as he didn't stink any more. He said he'd used that lotion, the one that's advertised, which he realizes now is no good, but he went for the girl in the ads. So I said after what I'd said, I owed him to give it a sniff, but I'd do it out in the park, on account if I had to throw up I could do it on the grass. So he said okay, and that's why we were there."

"And how *did* he smell, if I may ask?"

"Not good, but better. Enough, anyway, that I had to 'pologize for those various things I had said."

"Did he *'pologize* for raping you?"

"That subject didn't come up."

". . . Or did he?"

"Did he? Did he? Did he what?"

"Rape you?"

"I thought I told you he did."

"You did, and now I'm telling you, it's not true, what you've said—or if it is, it's not the whole truth, or even a fractional part of it. Sonya, on TV one night, in connection with White House stuff, I heard a guy say: 'The truth bears its own thumbprint, right in the middle of its forehead—and so does a lie, except bigger, from having a bigger thumb.' It's all a lie, what you've said, so maybe the other was too. Maybe it wasn't rape, maybe you weren't held by two kind friends of his. Who were they, anyway? Do you realize you've never said? And why didn't you tell your mother, until you got knocked up? Then, and then only, did you remember you were raped.

"You know what it reminds me of? Of Lincoln's story, of the man he was defending, as a lawyer, in Illinois, from a woman's charge that he raped her. She took the stand and he asked her: 'Madame, if it is true, as you say, that this defendant raped you on Tuesday afternoon, how come you didn't tell your husband till Friday night? 'Well I just didn't recollect,' she answered—and that's how it was with you!"

I could have said more, but didn't, and went back to my chair, where I slumped down, with no more steam in my boiler. She came over, knelt beside me, moistened her thumb, pressed it against her brow, and said: "I was raped—now what does the print say?"

"You were raped."

"Yes."

"Now rub again, for today."

She stared, then got up again, without rubbing, and went back to her place on the sofa. "Okay, it was the truth, every word, but not the whole truth, of course, so it was really a lie, with an extra big thumb. Gramie, what I left out was why. And that I'm not going to tell you. I told you before, our cloud went *pop,* soon as Miss Jane came back, so I know what I have to do, get out. And I'm going to. I said I wouldn't be inny pest, and I won't be, that I promise you. But I have something to do first, something that has to be done, and be done by me, as I was the cause of it all—and because I'm the one and the only one that can do it. So my time hasn't quite come. But until it comes, can I ask that you give me some peace? That you quit bugging me? I'm not going to lay up with Burl—maybe he thinks I am, but Burl can make a mistake. But I am going to use him, I hope, for what I must do, *what I must!*

"What I hafta!"

She almost screamed it, being suddenly all wrought up. I went over, sat down beside her, and took her in my arms. I whispered: "Fine, anything you say. But why do you have to go?"

"Because I love you is why."

Chapter 20

I reported to Mother next day, driving over there as soon as I'd checked in at the office. She listened and said: "Well I wouldn't know what to tell you—Sonya is smart, and I would swear she's decent, so she's not playing Burl's game, that we can be sure of. As to what game she *is* playing, I don't know how you find out, unless you hire a private detective, but not even he can tell you why, which is what you want to know."

We just sat for some time, and then she went on: "I can understand your upset, and I promise you, I'm on tension too. I haven't mentioned it to you, but Pat Moran called up, offering a piece of a deal he's putting together, a million-dollar apartment here in Riverdale—he's picked up five lots, three of them vacant, two with small houses on them, so on land he's okay. And as he means to build a garage behind his main building, no parking problem's involved, *and* as the apartments are going to be small, not suited to families with children, there'll be no strain on the school.

"Or in other words, it's a good, solid project that nobody should object to. Just the same, it calls for zoning reclassification, from Residential B to A—which is why he offered me in, as he counts on me to swing it. Well, I probably could. I've kept my connections up, and made a few new ones lately. But, until this thing is out of the way, I have no appetite for it. Politics is partly deals—like this one—but it's also partly combat. If you don't like a fight, stay out. I don't mind one, as a rule. But, with this thing hanging fire, I'm just a bundle of jitters. I can't forget what she said, about what's waiting for Jane—I feel as though a time-bomb were ticking somewhere. I told Pat include me out. I had to."

Some days went by, and then one night I went home, to have the door opened for me by Sonya, all dressed up in the same blue dress she'd had on the first day in the parking lot, and the little black hat, a tiny shell made of straw, on the order of a skull cap. I kissed her, followed her into the living room, looked her over and asked: "Well? We going out? Or what?"

"Why. . . I am. Yes."

"And I'm not?"

By that time, I had sat down on one of the sofas, and she sat opposite, across the table, on the other. She didn't answer at once, but then: "Gramie, my time has come."

"What the hell are you talking about?"

"I said I was going, didn't I? Well, now I am."

"But nobody's asked you to go."

"Listen, what's the good of staying? We've been all over that, over and over and over. No marriage can stand the strain when the wife comes between the guy and his dream, the guy and his million bucks. So, I'm shoving off, like I promised.

"But I thought it might be nice if we had a last dinner together, that we both could look back on and kind of keep in our hearts. So I got us a Beltsville turkey, and made hominy, rutabaga, and cranberry sauce to go with it—oh, and that Graves white wine that you like—it's all timed for seven-thirty, when it'll be getting dark and we can eat by candlelight. And talk about how nice things were when we were up on our cloud."

"Which is still up there, incidentally."

"No, it's not."

"It is, if you'd get on it, and . . ."

"Without the dream, it couldn't be, and isn't."

I went over, took her in my arms, and tried to carry her upstairs, but she wrestled me off, and I quit—but not till I noticed how soft she was, and warm, and part of me, somehow. She said, "Gramie, don't make it harder for me than it is. I don't want to go, God knows. I *have* to, that's all. So will you listen to me? What I've done today? So you can take up from where I left off and get the benefit?"

"What have you done today?"

"I broke up that marriage, Gramie."

"You mean Jane's? With Burl?"

"That's right."

"Then how did you break it up?"

"Does it matter? I did, that's all. It's what I've been hanging around for, what I had to do. Well? It's done, and there's no need to talk about it."

"There *is* need to talk."

"What's that supposed to mean?"

"You're keeping stuff back, stuff I have to know about."

"No, you don't."

"Sonya, what is this? What have you been up to?"

"I will not talk about it."

She went out to the kitchen and came back with the cocktail tray, making the martini at the side table. She chunked the ice with her pick, rubbed the glasses with lemon peel, put an olive with a toothpick in each, measured gin and vermouth with her eye. Then she dropped the ice in and stirred, till the pitcher began to smoke up. Then she poured and put my glass in front of me. I was still on her side of the table, and she sat down beside me. "I don't like it, but this once I'll drink with you, because it's our last night."

I raised my glass. "To us, then" I said.

"To us on our cloud when we had one."

We sipped and I sat there looking at her, thinking how pretty she was. She asked, "Can I go on?"

"If you insist, I can't stop you."

"First, about her, Mrs. Sibert—well, I keep calling her that, but she's really Mrs. Stuart, from being married to Burl. But, she's kicking him out—I imagine she already has. So, soon as I blow, get over there. Drive to her house, stretch her out on the floor, and give her what she wants from you—which was *her* dream all along, not this crazy thing with Burl. Then you'll get back *your* dream, and of course the million bucks. Be gentle with her, she'll cooperate."

"What else?"

"I'm taking the car you gave me."

"What else?"

"I'm keeping the thousand dollars that you put to my account, as I'm going to need it to live on, while I'm getting started again—I can get a job as a waitress, I'm pretty sure of that—but I don't want to feel afraid, or go home with my tail between my legs. So, I'm keeping that thousand, and some more I have too, that I *imbizzled* since we got married, from the household money you gave me. That's another thing I want to thank you for, how nice you treated me, giving me more than I needed—Gramie, you're one hell of a nice guy."

"Then what are you leaving me for?"

"I said. It's not a what, it's a who. Mrs. Sibert."

"What else?"

"Did you hear me? I *imbizzled* four hundred dollars."

"Sonya, I love you."

"Well? I love you. It's why I'm leaving."

"How about one last trip on our cloud?"

"If I took it I couldn't go."

"That's the whole idea."

"No, Gramie! I must go! I hafta."

It was getting dark, and she took the tray to the kitchen, along with both our glasses. Then she tinkled her bell and called, and I went back to the dining room. The table was beautifully set, with roses as a centerpiece, arranged flat in a glass dish, a candle on each side, and tomato salad waiting, ready to eat. When we'd finished it she took the plates and brought in the turkey, a cute little one, perfectly cooked. Then she brought the hominy and rutabaga and cranberry sauce, and I did the carving.

She served me my giblet sauce, correcting me when I called it giblet gravy. She said: "It's sauce, not gravy—I made it as it says in *Joy of Cooking*. It's more digestible than gravy, and tastes better." Then she poured the wine. Graves is a wine I like, a Bordeaux white, fairly dry, with a trace of sweet—but what I liked most about it was that she liked it too.

For dessert she served ice cream bricks with brandied cherries. Then for the grand finale, she served *coffee diable,* lighting it, and blowing the candles out. In the blue flame she looked like a girl from some kind of dream world, and I wanted to cry. "What's the matter?" she asked.

"I love you."

"Then, we love each other."

I went in the living room, where in a few minutes she joined me, carrying her handbag and little spring coat. I must have had a look on my face as she dropped them on a chair, and said, "Well? My other things, my bags and stuff, are all packed and in the car." She sat beside me on my sofa, giving me all sorts of directions about the turkey, the hominy and how to cook it, or warm it up, or whatever I was supposed to do with it, and I guess I listened, though I haven't the faintest idea what she said. Then she stopped and pulled my arm around her and started inhaling me. "If only you didn't smell so nice," she whispered. "Now kiss me. Kiss me good-bye."

I kissed her. I held her close, so close I meant never to let her loose. She didn't seem to mind, but kissed back, so our lips were glued. That's when the doorbell rang. "Oh for Christ's sake!" I growled.

"You better see who it is."

"To hell with them – let them go away."

"Want me to go, Gramie?"

"I'll do it."

I went to the door. Jane Sibert was there.

Chapter 21

If there was anyone I wanted to see just then, I can't think now who it was, but if there was one person on earth I certainly did not want to see, it had to be her. And apparently, she felt the same about me. She had on a spring coat, much like Sonya's, and a white dress that went nice with her soft blue hair, but her eyes were hard, and looked away as soon as she saw me. She said: "Good evening, Gramie, I hope you've been well. I'm calling on Mrs. Kirby, if she's at home."

I asked her in and said I'd see, but almost at once Sonya was there, with a bright, chirpy greeting. "Why Miss Jane," she sang out, "what a nice *co-instance*. I was fixing to go see you, to drive out to your place, later on in the evening. And so you saved me the trouble. Why don't we go in and sit down." Sonya led the way to the living room, sat Jane down on a sofa, took the other one herself, and waited till I camped on a chair, before asking: "What brings you, Miss Jane? What can I do for you?"

"So! It *was* you!"

Jane whispered it dramatically, but Sonya drew a blank, and gave it a long stare. "*Who* was me?" she asked.

"That girl who was there. Burl said it was, and..."

"Well of course! I should have said who I was."

"You ladies know each other?" I enquired.

"Know each other!" said Sonya. "I'll say we do."

She started to talk, in the airiest kind of way, as though telling a funny story, which I suppose in a way it was. "Well," she said, speaking mainly to me, but turning to Jane now and then, as though for corroboration, "I mentioned, I think, that I busted her marriage up, *and* so long as she's here, there's no harm in saying how. I did it by working on Burl, the well-known weakness he has, of chasing skirts any age, so all I had to do was shake mine at him once, and sure enough here he came running.

"So he kept asking me up for a date in that office he has, and I kept putting him off. So then I said I would, but the thing of it was I didn't trust him, any more than I'd trust any man: that he would be on time, and not give me some kind of a stand-up, so I'd have to wait in the hall. I said give me a key, so I can go in at once, soon as I come to the door, and wait inside; then he'd have a date. So he did.

"So soon as I checked that it really was the right key, and not some kind of a cross he'd handed me, I had a duplicate made, and mailed one to her, in Hyattsville. Care General Delivery there, so it couldn't be innercepted by Burl out at the house. So soon as she picked it up, after I rang her about it, I lined the stakeout up. I told her come in on us three-fifteen today, and had everything ready, what she was going to find. Well say," she said to Miss Jane, "you were long enough coming—it was three-thirty and then some before I heard the click of your key turning the lock."

"Anyway, I came," said Miss Jane, very grim.

"Okay. So what are you doing here?"

Sonya wasn't quite so airy now, but Miss Jane snapped

back at her: "I told you already—I had to make sure who you were, that Burl was telling the truth!"

"But that's not all, is it?"

". . . I beg your pardon, Mrs. Kirby?"

"Now that I've busted your marriage up—at lease as I hope I have—you think you'll do the same for me. Well I have news for you: My marriage is already busted. I was on my way out, the moment you rang the bell. So you have a clear track with Gramie, and I heartily wish you well. So now . . ."

She picked up her coat and bag, but Jane, who'd been deflated a bit, tried to blow herself up again. "I caught her!" she screamed. "In the act!"

"Now, Miss Jane, not that. Not quite."

"In the act! *He had exposed himself!*"

She repeated it, and I cut in, to Sonya, "Just a minute, please. What does that mean, 'He had exposed himself'?"

"Means he had his thing hanging out—I guess that's what it means. Yeah, it's how he makes his pass—we're supposed to fall in a faint, all us girls are, from the joy of looking at it. Well? It's how he got *her*"—jerking her thumb at Miss Jane—"that first night at your mother's when they ran into each other there, and she 'sisted on riding him home. But then when they got there, to the Stuart Building, he wouldn't get out of the car, said she was all wrought up and he was going to see *her* home.

"So he did, and when she brought him inside—lo and behold—he unzipped, took it out, and asked if she wanted to play with it. So she said no, but let on she'd like to fondle it. Well that hit Burl funny, for some reason, and I guess it does me, a little bit. Anyway, when she'd fondled on it awhile, she thought of a place to put it, and did, right there on the parlor floor, in under the whispering cattails. Where the cattails come in, I wouldn't personally know, but that's how Burl told it to me, and I aim to be truthful, always."

Jane, having blown herself up for a moment, made a weak shrivel. When Sonya started her airy recital, she covered her face with her hands, and then, as it went on, pulled her knees up under her chin, and toppled over sidewise, against the end of the sofa, so she was just a small pile of clothing, a tiny, collapsed old woman, shaking and shivering and shuddering.

Sonya went over to her, and wound up: "Miss Jane, we don't happen to have a hole that you can crawl into, but you can make out, I reckon, with a pillow over your head." So she put a sofa pillow on Jane's head, and turned away, as though from a deed well done.

"What are you putting on your head?" I snarled, sounding thick and mean and ugly.

"Well I'm wearing a hat," she snapped.

"You damned cheap twerp, how can you stand there, and talk about 'his thing,' as though it meant nothing at all?"

"Well it didn't—except to make me sick, for reasons I already said. But listen, I knew about it! It's not like I had to be scared, or . . ."

"Will you shut up about it?"

"Then okay, we say no more."

"Because I just don't care to think what he may have been doing with it to have it hanging out in such fashion."

"Oh, so that's what's bugging you?"

"It may not seem like much, but —— "

"I have proof he didn't do innything!"

"Produce the proof. *Now!*"

So she did, a lot quicker than I expected. She just flipped up her dress, and there around her waist, over her panty hose, like a belt, was a length of shiny chain, about the size of tire chain, and between her legs, like a G-string, was another. Fastening the chains together was a little brass padlock. "My *ceinture de chastité*," she explained, but called it *cincher de chastity*. "They had them in olden times, we read about them in school—it's where *cinch* comes from, the thing you put on a horse. I had it on when I went to his office, and if he could have got through it, he's a better man than I think—but things didn't get that far. They made it for me at College Park Hardware, cutting the chain to my measure, and being somewhat amused when I told them the idea of it. It's not too comfortable, but I left it on tonight as I expected to go to Miss Jane's, and I decided to take no chances, as Burl might have been there too."

She took a key ring from her bag, found a key, unlocked the little brass padlock, and took both chains off, putting them in her bag. "My, that feels good!" she exclaimed. "What a relief."

"I think it's time you went."

"I'll decide when I go!" She came over and slapped my face. "For the two hundredth time: I'm your wife and this is my home—you're not putting me out and nobody's putting me out, except me, when I'm ready to go!"

"As soon as you're ready, I am."

"Well I'm not, not yet."

She went to Jane, lifted the pillow, and shook her. "Miss Jane," she said, "I'm sorry, but there's things I must say to you."

Jane sat up, a broken, shamed old woman. "First," Sonya went on, "Dale Morgan—does that name mean something to you?"

"I suppose so," Jane answered dully. "Yes."

"You know how she died?"

"In some sort of accident I heard."

"Burl killed her, is how."

Jane, who until now had taken no interest, opened her eyes wide. "What did you say, Mrs. Kirby?" she asked, very sharp.

"I said Burl Stuart killed her, in some slick way he alone could explain, for insurance he carried on her, fifty thousand dollars, which was paid—and which you've been living on, since you've been married to him. Miss Jane, here's what I'm leading to: Burl Stuart means to kill *you,* for the land you've made him heir to, in that will you let him have, worth twenty times what he made on Dale. Miss Jane, you're not to use your car, or go home, or give him inny kind of chance, to do to *you* what he did to *Dale.* And on top of that, right away quick, you must see your lawyer, have him do what it takes to cancel that will Burl has, so it's not in effect inny more, and so he *knows* you're no longer worth to him more dead than you are alive. Don't tell him he must send it back—wild horses couldn't make him, you'll have to do more than that, your lawyer can tell you what. I would think draw a new will, maybe making Gramie your heir, as he was before and should have been all along—but that's up to you, of course. Do you hear what I say, Miss Jane? Am I getting through to you?"

"I don't believe one word."

"You and the undertaker, you're quite a pair, you are—*he* don't take nobody's word. He don't have to."

That seemed to reach Jane as nothing had until then, and Sonya went on: "I'm going now, so the coast is clear, for tonight. If I were you, I'd stay here if Gramie is willing—crawl in his bed and let nature take its course. Miss Jane, it just might. Because pay no attention to what Burl said, about Gramie not being normal—he's just as normal as you are, maybe more so, being thirty years younger." And, as Jane flinched: "Well I'm sorry if you don't like it, but you haven't been nice to me, spite of all I've been doing for you. So maybe I don't mind cutting you up. Excuse me."

Still carrying the coat and bag, she went scampering out to the kitchen, and for some minutes I sat with Jane, who began pulling herself together. Then, in a nervous but conversational tone she asked me: "Could *any of that* be true?"

"Jane, all of it's true."

"You're not serious?"

"Jane, Burl means to kill you!"

At last, she seemed to get through her head that it wasn't a game of some kind that Sonya had been playing, or a contest in nasty remarks, or something of that kind. She began gasping, as fear started to talk, and of all the things that can talk, I guess fear says it plainer. She sat there, trying for control, and occasionally massaging her lips, that sure sign of terror. Then she jumped up, saying: "I have to know more about this!" and went running out to the kitchen. Once or twice she called "Mrs. Kirby!" and then came stumbling back, a baffled look on her face. "She's not there!" she said. "She's not anywhere around."

A horrible, frightening suspicion crept in on me, as I went charging back to the kitchen, whispering: "Sonya! Sonya, where are you?" But she wasn't there, though the kitchen was in apple pie order. I went out back and called, looked for her car in the drive, then went out front and looked. It wasn't there, it wasn't anywhere. I let myself in the front door, went back in with Jane and sat down. She stared at me but nothing was said. Pretty soon the phone rang and I answered.

"Gramie?" said Sonya, very soft and friendly. "I'm at People's. I called to say good-bye and blow you a kiss on the phone. I couldn't have kissed you just now, not with her looking on." She said more, but I kept cutting in, begging her to come back, saying I hadn't meant it, what I'd told her before she went, and all kinds of stuff of that kind, and God knows I meant every word. But she kept holding to it, that she'd left me, that she was going away, that I mustn't try to find out where she was or what she was doing. Then, saying she'd call now and then, "To see how you're getting along," she blew me the kiss and hung up.

Back in the living room, I sat for some moments with Jane staring at me. "You love her?" she asked, pretty soon.

"I'm nuts about her. She's part of me."

"I have to be going now."

"Where?" I snapped. "Didn't you hear what she said?"

"Well I can't stay here, that's certain!"

She was a little hysterical about it, and I took her back over it once, what Sonya had explained to her, why she couldn't go home, why she had to go someplace where she'd be safe from Burl. All of a sudden I went to the phone and dialed Mother. "Can you put Jane up for one night?" I asked her.

"Put up with her, I think you mean!"

"Okay, call it that, but something has happened."

"Is she there?"

"I'll see if she wants to talk."

Jane talked, like a schoolgirl holding her hand out to be blistered with a ruler. Then she motioned me back to the phone, and Mother said: "All right, send her over." But instead, I took her over, on the way explaining to her what she had to do with her car: Have the garage men come and get it, first explaining to them it had better be towed, else the steering might go haywire, and she understood all right, as she collapsed into tears in the middle of it, and kept moaning: "I'm so scared! Oh, Gramie, I'm so scared."

Mother was cool at first, but then suddenly warmed, when she saw the state she was in, and took her upstairs to bed. When she came down I explained, at least a little of it, what had happened today and tonight, and she stood there shaking her head. "Will I ever hear the end? Will there be any end to this mess?"

I didn't have an answer to that.

It was going on twelve when I headed home once more, to enter the bleakest house, and start the blackest night, that any man ever faced.

Chapter 22

The next six weeks were a mockery. Everything broke for me, in a material way, and also broke for Mother, but everything else went flooey.

In business I got a break from the F.X. Reilly Estate, which retained me to sell ten houses, rental jobs in West Hyattsville, running $20,000 apiece. It was a $200,000 deal, and I tore in, of course. I didn't stampede, just took it one house at a time, but in a month, believe it or not, I'd got rid of them all. I rated a bonus and got it, and had reason to feel proud—but didn't feel anything. Because Sonya was calling by now, every two or three nights, very friendly, wanting to know how things were, and I begged her, pleaded over the phone, to come back to me, but she wouldn't.

The worst of it was, I didn't know where she was, but suspected it was Reno. And what really made it bad was that her mother knew. She was calling Mrs. Lang too, and Mrs. Lang would call me, in a friendly way, just wishing she could tell me where Sonya was, but of course couldn't, as she was pledged not to. That's nice, when your mother-in-law knows where your wife is staying, and you don't. So maybe she'd break if you coaxed, and give you a little hint, but fat chance of that, really.

And on Mother's end, she picked up an ace when Mort Leonard, Jane's lawyer, heard of her bust-up with Burl, and realized what it could mean—perhaps having his own opinion of Burl to start with, and perhaps having heard a few rumors. Anyway, it seems that to revoke one will you have to draw another, but in whose favor was the question Jane was faced with. So, for various reasons, there could be only one answer, and she was back once more to Mother. That put the dream back on its feet, but I took no interest and neither did she.

"I'm sick of it!" she burst out, in my office one day. "Of her, of her land, of Burl—especially of him! Gramie, he's been calling up, since Mort wrote him about it, about this new will that she's drawn, so he'd know the old one was void, the one that she drew in his favor—he's been ringing me late at night, saying horrible things. I wouldn't put anything past him! *Anything!*"

And then something happened that pretty well proved she wasn't imagining things. Jane had put her car in storage, after what Sonya had said, had it towed to Clint Jervis's lot, intending to have it checked, but putting it off for some reason. So Clint's boy Rod began borrowing it, to ride his girl around, and one night the steering went haywire and dumped them in the ditch. Rod and the girl weren't hurt, but the car was a total wreck, as Jane learned next morning, when the insurance office called. Mother called me and I went over, and I'm telling you, we all looked at each other, and knew what the answer was.

My birthday, as a rule, hasn't meant much to me, though of course, people make it pleasant, and you get a bit of a bang. But this year, for some reason, I kept thinking about it, the contrast it would be with the one I had last year, my thirtieth. That day had been wonderfully pleasant—a quickie visit from Lynn, a necktie from Jane, a party at my mother's later in the evening. Even the weather had helped. My birthday's September 12, Old Defender's Day, as it's called here in Maryland, when Fort McHenry held out, and *The Star-Spangled Banner* was born. It's the end of summer, the beginning of fall, with the smell of Concord grapes, like winy perfume, hanging in the air. You could smell them all over that day, and if I wasn't perfectly happy, at least I was enjoying life, which until Sonya came along, was all I really asked.

But now it was all different. There was no winy smell, as the day was overcast, and the air felt raw. Helen Musick had remembered, and given me a bottle of lotion, and Mother of course had called—but she said nothing about coming over, and no wonder, with Jane in the house all the time. I got home around six, feeling utterly depressed, because all I could think of was Sonya, and how I wished she was there. I parked in the drive, slipped the lotion in my pocket, went up to the door, put my key in and unlocked, feeling as glum as I'd ever felt in my life.

But as soon as I opened the door a terrific surprise was there, a big birthday cake on the telephone table, with a flock of candles burning, thirty-one as I knew without counting. And then at once, from the living room, came the chords on the piano, *Happy Birthday to You*. It played almost to the end, and then a small thready girl's voice sang: *Happy Birthday, Dear Gramie, Happy Birthday to You!* For a few terrible seconds I wasn't quite sure, as I'd never heard her sing. But then in the arch there she was, flinging herself into my arms, burrowing her nose into my shirt, drawing deep, trembly breaths. Then our mouths came together in a long, beautiful kiss. I lifted her, so her feet swung clear of the floor, and carried her into the living room. I sat down in one of the chairs, pulled her onto my lap, and kept right on kissing her, holding her close, and patting her. After a long time our mouths pulled apart, and little by little, though still trembling, we were able to talk. I said: "So – so – and so. You came."

"I had to, I couldn't help it."

"Well? I told you, didn't I? If you had to be Little Miss Fixit, okay – but everything's fixed. So what were you waiting for?"

"How do you mean, everything's fixed?"

"Well I told you, last time you called!"

"Yes, but I didn't get it straight."

"Well, first off, Jane moved in with Mother."

"When was this?"

"That same night. When you scared her to death."

"Then she didn't stay with you?"

"You think I'd let her?"

"Well after all she had the land."

"Yeah, but now she's left it to Mother. She's not mad at her any more. She realizes. Or whatever the hell she does. If you ask me she's somewhat balmy."

"About you, she is."

"Was. She came to her senses, I think."

"More'n I did. I'm still balmy about you."

"Mutual. Likewise. Vice versa. Kiss me."

She kissed me, and some little time went by. "Gramie, don't you know why I came?"

"I'll bite. Why?"

"That beautiful wire you sent me."

Now if I could say I reacted to that in a way that made some sense, or that showed I had some brains, or that did me credit in any way, I certainly would – but I can't. All I felt was put out, or bored, or annoyed, that something apart from us was edging in between, to louse up our moment, and my only clear idea was to give it some kind of brush, so we could go on as we had been going, with kisses, pats, and talk about being balmy. I said: "Uh-huh."

"Didn't you hear what I said, Gramie?"

"Somebody sent you a wire."

"*You* sent me a wire!"

Then, and then only, at last, not caring much, or wanting to talk about it: "I'm sorry, I didn't send any wire."

"Well you certainly did!"

She jumped up, went to the side table, opened her bag, took out a yellow telegram, and brought it over to me. It was a night letter, a long one, leading off about my birthday, quoting *The Star-Spangled Banner,* and saying all I wanted to see by the dawn's early light was her head on the pillow beside me—and more of the same, quite poetic. It begged her to come home and help me celebrate, and wound up: *"Love Love Love, Gramie."*

I said: "I know nothing about it."

She took it, crossed to a sofa and collapsed into tears. I went over, folded her in, and asked, "Is it all that important? So somebody sent you a wire, but all it said was what I've been trying to say over the phone a hundred times, whenever you called, that you should come back to me, back to your home."

"But that wire is why I came."

"I thought *I* was why you came."

"I thought you sent it is why. It's why I got shook."

"If I'd known where you were, I'd have sent you a hundred wires, but I didn't, you didn't tell me. You told your mother, and she told the Hyattsville Post Office—but she wouldn't tell me, you forbade her."

"I was so thrilled, you finding out where I was."

"Well you can knock it off with those shakes, as I didn't lift a finger to find out where you were, and wouldn't. I have some pride left, I hope."

"Now we'll have to start over."

"How, start over?"

"I've just said. It's why I came. But now——!"

"Yes, I think you're right—a completely fresh start is

what's called for. I'll mumble under your ear—work around to your mouth—then carry you up—and we'll see if our cloud is still there."

I started off, and just then the chimes in the hall sounded. I said: "I've never known it to fail that when we get in sight of our cloud, the goddam doorbell rings."

I got up and started for the hall. Then: *"Gramie!"* she burst out, in a voice like a whipcrack. *"I've just waked up! Don't answer! Don't do it! Don't open that door!"*

By then she was beside me, her eyes big and almost black. I said, "At least we can see who it is."

I opened the pigeonhole and a man was there, in red jacket and Afro hairdo. I opened the door, asked: "Yes? What is it?"

He didn't answer me, but cocked a gun in my stomach, a big, shiny, stainless steel thing, almost a submachine gun, and motioned to my hands. I put them up and he stepped inside, closing the door behind him. I said: "Okay, take it easy, just say what it is, and that's how it's going to be. I have money, and I'll hand it over, but first lower that gun—this girl is my wife and I don't want her hurt. And, to get out my wallet, I have to lower my hands, so——"

But he motioned again and I had to keep my hands up. Suddenly she said, "Gramie, it's Burl—in that mask he brought home from Japan and the Afro wig that goes with it."

"We can't fool little Bright Eyes."

He took off the wig, dropped it in the chair beside the phone table, then pulled off the mask, which was of some sort of thin rubber, with eye, nose, and mouth holes, and went on like scuba gear, and suddenly was my brother, with his same little twitchy grin that was more like a sneer.

"That feels better," he remarked, very breezy, dropping the mask on top of the wig. "Stuff like that can be hot, this time of year."

"Did you send me that wire?"

"Come to think of it, Sonya, I may have."

"You had a nerve."

"Well? I heard Gramie was pining for you, and of course I was. So, two birds with one stone, and after all it was you."

"What do you mean, you were pining for me?"

"Well what do you think?"

"What do you want?"

"Two or three things, all at the same time, but I'll be very glad to explain—in fact, I want to explain, I want you to get very clear, what I'm doing here. Shall we go in and sit down?"

"Who wants to know?"

For some reason, it infuriated me, on top of everything else, that this jerk should be inviting us into the sitting room, as though he owned the joint. I said, "This is our house, and we do the inviting around here!"

"Not when I hold the gun."

Chapter 23

He stepped behind me, slapped my pockets, and then repeated that we should "go in and sit down." Sonya and I, walking beside each other, led the way to the living room, with him behind us, holding the gun. He said, "Okay, Gramie, I'll take this sofa, and you and Sonya can sit on the other, but"—pointing to the cocktail table between the two sofas—"will you move this table out, so there's nothing in between? So I can look up Sonya's legs and see what she's got?" I told him to watch his language, and he told me do as he said, but with a sudden, half hysterical note in his voice that betrayed the state he was in. I moved the table a few feet, and he said: "That's good. Now sit down." I sat and he turned to Sonya. "Okay," he said, "take 'em off."

". . . Take what off?"

"Drawers. Panty hose. Whatever they are."

"And suppose I don't?"

"Then I will. But I might do it kind of rough."

He lifted her skirt as though to show her, but she slapped his hand away. "Keep your hands off me!" she snapped. "How many times do I have to tell you? You stink. You smell like feet that haven't been washed—or more like a dead rat, maybe."

"I never smelled feet that haven't been washed—my friends all wash their feet, and I've never even *seen* a dead rat, let alone smelled one—I hope you tell me some day where you were raised, Sonya, that you know so much about it, how feet and dead rats smell. But just right now, skip it! Quit stalling! Take 'em off, I said!"

She stepped out of her shoes, and with him still pawing at her, slipped off her panty hose. She dropped them on the table, stooped, and put her shoes on again. He said: "Sit down!"

She sat.

He sat, and slouched over to peep.

"Open your legs."

She opened her legs.

He stared, his lips slimy wet. Then, though it cost him an effort, taking his eyes off her, he started to talk. "So what do I want? Like I said, two or three things, but let's take them one at a time. But before I get to them, there's something I want you to know: I heard what you said to Gramie, that he shouldn't open that door—but don't hold it against him, that he did what you told him not to. It wouldn't have been any different—I have a key, and would have come in, irregardless. That's the first thing I want to make clear: I'm playing it back just as you played it at me, key and all—I got mine from your cleaning woman, with the same song-and-dance, pretending I wanted a date, like you pretended to me, that day when you staked me out, broke up my marriage, and cut me out of my land, that I was due to inherit——"

"After you knocked her off."

"Knocked who off?"

"Your wife, who do you think?"

"My, my, my, the way you talk! Well, speaking of knocking off, that brings up the subject of Gramie."

"In what way, the subject of Gramie?"

"I'm playing it back at him, just as he played it to me, that day when he hit me, sneaked a punch when I wasn't looking—and kicked me, when I was down. I'll do the same, except perhaps harder."

"And then what?"

"Hey, not so fast. Other stuff comes first!"

"Come on, spit it out! What are you up to?"

"Before I attend to him, there's what I do to you—with him looking on. Last time we had two, this time only one—but he's your husband, and so it equalizes."

"And then what?"

"I attend to *him,* with *you* looking on."

"And then what?"

"Well Sonya, that would be up to you."

"Come on, jerk, say what you mean!"

"I did say it, *it would be up to you!* My mother's hell-bent for history, says I'm a cut-rate Casanova, or something, so I'll spout some history too. You can be Mary, Queen of Scots—who held still for her husband's murder, and lived happily ever afterward."

"Until they chopped off her head."

"Well anyway, she lived, at least for a while."

"You think I'd hold still for Gramie's murder?"

"Well if you don't, dead wives tell no tales."

"And you think your mother'll hold still?"

To that he made no answer, being caught by surprise. She jumped up and tore in, half screaming: "You think she won't guess who killed her favorite child, her first-born, the apple of her eye? You think she won't know who the black man was, that she won't see inny connection between him and that Japanese mask, or the Afro wig that you had? You think she's not going to use it, the clout she has in this county? The political stuff she can pull? Burl, she hates your guts, and you're looking hell in the face right now, if you have the sense to know it! You . . ."

"Shut up! Take off your clothes!"

"Let's see you take 'em off me!"

He began answering what she'd said, about Mother, by reciting his alibi, the one he had fixed up, down at the Bijou Theatre, where he'd dated up the cashier, after the early show, where "I'm inside at this very minute, as nobody saw me go out, through the fire door at the side, or will see me go back in—" and more of the same, all the while facing her, as they stood almost belly to belly, there in front of me, in between the sofas. But there was something he forgot, which was what she really was, a teenage brat who kicked, as she often did me. So she kicked him right now, so fast you could hardly see it, but not in the stomach, her usual place, but in a much tenderer spot, so he jackknifed. I jacked-in-the-boxed, jumping up as though on springs, grabbing the gun, twisting it out of his hand. Suddenly it was a whole new ballgame.

I backed him to the hall, with her walking beside me, whispering wonderful things, about how proud we could be of each other, for what we'd done together, and I guess I whispered back—it looks as though I must have. Then all of a sudden she said, out loud so he could hear her: "Gramie, give me the gun and I'll hold it—then you beat him up, like you did that other time, except now you really beat him up, so his face is just a jelly, and he stays that way for a while. *That'll* settle his hash, so we see the end of him!"

"Sonya, will you call the police?"

"The police? *The police?*"

"Of course—eight-six-four, seven thousand!"

"But suppose he talks? Suppose it's a mess?"

"If he talks, he'll be putting himself behind bars, which

is just where I want to see him. . . . It's what your father wanted to do! For once we could do the right thing, and listen to him!"

"My father wanted to kill him."

"Oh that'll be a help, if a mess is what we want!"

I waited, but instead of calling, she began blowing out the candles, which were pretty well burned down, but still lit, on the cake. She blew out two or three, and on the next puff got two or three more. But I jerked her back to the phone, said: *"Sonya! Will you—for God's sake—call?"*

At last, she left off with the candles and started to dial. We were standing there, all three of us, so close you could have covered us with an umbrella—she at the edge of the table, having pushed the chair to one side; he sat at the table too, within a few inches of her; I in front of him, the gun pressed to his gut. I didn't see him move. I must have been looking at her, so I'd taken me eye off him. And I didn't see the flame—at least, at first I didn't. What I saw was her mouth, as it opened when she screamed. Then I heard her hair kind of crackle as it caught fire. Then at last I saw the flame, where she was smacking it out, or trying to smack it out, with her hand, on her bottom. I grabbed her, lifted, and flung her to the floor, to get her horizontal, so I could smack out the fire with my hand, which I did. Then I smacked at the cake, on the table, to put out the candles, at last. Then I held her close, kissing her, and whispering: "I had to—it's how you do, when somebody catches on fire, it's the only way!"

She was moaning in pain, but nodded. All that took, I suppose, three seconds, but it seemed more like a year, and I give you one guess, when I looked, who was holding the gun. He was completely unexcited, as calm as a wooden Indian, but seemed to be waiting for something. Pretty soon, in a minute or so, here it came: the ring of the phone. He told her: "Answer it, Sonya. And see that you talk right!"

"Answer it: How can I talk? I'm hurt! I'm burned!"

"I said answer it. Now!"

I started to argue with him, to curse at him, to bawl him out, but she said: "No, Gramie, no – or he'll kill us."

She scrambled to her feet, me helping her, while the phone bell went right on. Then she answered, in a chirpy, conversational way, kind of teary, but not much: "Hello? . . . Oh. Mrs. Persoff – I'm sorry I took so long, but I was out in the kitchen . . . Yes, I did scream, I certainly did – after doing the stupidest thing! It's Mr. Kirby's birthday, and I got him a cake, with candles. I was just blowing them out, when I stepped too close and my sleeve caught. . . . No, it's not bad, but I could have burned myself, I could really have done myself in. . . . Oh, no thank you, Mrs. Persoff, Mr. Kirby is fixing me up – I'm not dressed, and you'd just be complicating things for me. But thank you ever so much."

She hung up. He said: "I told you, take it off."

"Take what off?"

"The dress! Whatever you've got!"

"How can I? It's stuck to me, where you set me on fire, like a rat! Listen, I need a doctor! I can't — "

"Take it off!"

She took it off, loosening the places that were stuck, two patches on her hip, and lifting it over her head. She was stark naked except for the shoes, and livid red blotches showed, on her shoulder, hip, and neck. All around the place on her neck was a mass of singed black hair. He said: "Get in that closet."

She stepped in the hall closet, the one I had for guests' coats and hats. He closed the door and turned the key in the lock. To me he said, "Face the wall."

I faced the wall.

"Put your hands flat against it."

I put my hands flat against it.

Something crashed on my head.

I didn't come to all at once, only little by little. First I felt pain, a jolting pain in my back, as though something was hitting me. I tried to fend it off, but couldn't move my hand. Then I realized it was tied, that both my hands were tied behind my back. I didn't know with what, but it turned out later it was with kitchen towels, knotted hard and wetted, to set the cloth. Then, as I tried to move, I found my feet were tied, too. The jolts to my back kept on, and suddenly I heard her scream: "Stop it! Stop it, I tell you! You stop kicking him, do you hear me?"

"I kick him where he kicked me."

"You could kill him, doing that!"

"Oh wouldn't that be awful!"

That went on for some time, a couple of years, so it seemed, with me flopping around, straining to pull loose. Then my shoulder was jerked to flop me on my back instead of my stomach. When at last I opened my eyes, the two of them were there, she naked as before, the red blotches bigger it seemed, and he naked too, except for underpants. He had her by the wrist, yanking her around, and the sight of it made me furious, but I couldn't get loose to stop it. They wrestled around, she trying to break away, he trying to make her hold still, and each stomp of their feet shook the floor, so I felt it in my head, which wanted to split. I realized pretty soon that he didn't have the gun, that he'd put it on a chair, and that that was what she was doing, trying to pull clear and get to it. But he flung her clear and picked it up. "Now," he snarled. "Quit fooling around, get on the floor."

"I will in a pig's eye."

He corrected her, with words I don't put in, and she agreed, repeating them back at him, and twisting them around, so they applied to him. She turned and went to the side table, and he asked: "What are you doing there?"

"Getting a napkin, stupid. "Maybe I have to get raped, but let's not mess up my rug. It's a beautiful thing, and Gramie takes pride in his house."

"Goddam it, okay."

She faced him again, the napkin over one arm, and he beckoned her to him. He said: "I told you, get on the floor."

"And I told you, I won't."

Then, in a saucy, come-get-me way, she sashayed up to him. But to grab her he had to put down the gun, which he did, once more, in the chair. She said: "You poor cripple, you had to have help before, two people to hold me for you, do you think you can rape me now, with no one to help you at all? Oh boy, is that a joke."

It seemed funny, after saying that, that she didn't duck to make him catch her. However, she didn't. She just stood there, smiling to show her teeth, and then came marching to him, both her hands held out, the napkin flapping in one. He grabbed at her, and she slapped with her free hand, fired one right at his face. He grabbed it with both hands. Then began a waltz that made no sense, with him staggering around, his hands gripping his side, and her staggering with him, beating with her fist at something inside the napkin. It went on a long time, or what seemed a long time to me, with each lurch and jerk and stomp shaking the floor under my head. But then, just for a glimpse I saw red under the napkin, but not the red of blood. It was the red of the ice-pick butt, and I knew then what she had done—chocked that ice pick into him, that she'd got when she got the napkin, and hidden inside its folds when she turned away from the table. She was hammering the butt into him, while he fought to pull it out. Then suddenly he gasped, went straight up in the air, and came down in a heap on the floor.

My head almost split, and red flame shot in front of my eyes.

Chapter 24

Next, I didn't know where I was, or when it was, or who I was, or anything, except that I was awake, and was somewhere. When I opened my eyes I seemed to be in a bed, though in what bed I had no idea, as it looked quite strange to me. Then I caught sight of a tube that ran down to my arm from a bottle up above me somewhere. Then, in a chair a few feet away, I could see Sonya, in a blue gingham dress looking very sloppy, the upper part unbuttoned, head twisted around and her mouth open. If I made some noise I don't know, but suddenly her eyes opened and she looked at me, apparently in surprise. Then she got up and came over, staring down at me. Then she started to cry and picked up my hand, kissing it over and over. Then she knelt beside me, putting her face in the covers and starting to whisper, I thought in prayer.

And not to string it out, what she was praying about, she was offering thanks to God, that at last I'd come to, that I *could* look at her and know her. Because I'd been in a coma for days, from that crack on the head Burl gave me with the butt of his gun, so nobody really knew, not even the doctors, if I'd come out of it or not. When I did was when she cracked up, and took it out praying. Except for that, the whispering she did to God, I don't remember anything said.

Next thing I knew it was night, with a dim light somewhere, and Sonya still there, though not in a different dress. But also with her was Mother, in a black instead of her usual red, holding her hand. Pretty soon her eye caught mine and she waved, twinkling her fingers at me. I twinkled my fingers back. It seemed to startle Sonya, and she gripped Mother's arm. "Hey!" I said. "That's my mother—can't I wave at her?"

"Honey," she whispered, coming close to the bed. "Of course you can wave at her—that you *can* wave's the wonderful part—no one was sure that you would, never. That you wouldn't be paralyzed."

"Yes, Gramie, I'm shook," said Mother.

"Then I'll make it unanimous."

I laughed, but then suddenly sobs were shaking me, and Mother said: "He's weak, that's all. Gramie, take it easy, don't try to talk."

"It's not weakness, it's *her.*" I pointed at Sonya. "She got burned, where that rat set her on fire. What about that?" I asked her.

"Second degree, is all. I'm blistered but won't be scarred." Then she lifted a ribbon she had on her hair, to show me her neck, which was red with white blisters on it, and then hiked up her dress, to show me her bottom, which was also blistered. I said: "It's still the prettiest backside that ever was on this earth."

"They don't bandage a burn inny more," said Sonya. "They leave it so the air can get in. They put stuff on it, though."

Then it was morning, and a nurse was there, a girl in green uniform, with a glass of orange juice. "What?" I said. "No eggs? No bacon? No toast? What is this, Starvation Hall?"

"You think you can eat all that?"

"Try me."

She went back, then came in with a full tray, and I started wolfing it down. An intern came in and watched me. Then: "I don't see any need for more intravenous feeding," he said. "I think he can do without *this.*" He pulled a glass pin from my arm, that the tube was connected to, and took the bottle down. About that time Sonya came in, saw the tube in his hand, and the breakfast tray. Right away she started to cry.

Then the girl washed me and bathed me and changed me, and I was alone once more with Sonya, but for the first time I was myself and not just talking along but not knowing right from left. I asked: "Honey, where am I?"

"Prince Georges General."

"And how long have I been here?"

"Six days."

"*. . . Six days?*"

"Gramie, the longest days of my life—they didn't have inny end, because none of these doctors knew if you were going to live. Once you did die—your heart stopped, right there on the bed, and hadn't been for that doctor, the one who took your tube, you'd have been carried out feet first. I saw your jaw drop and called him, and he massaged your chest. I thought he'd rub all the skin off, but at last your face twitched, and you breathed. That was after they operated—you've been trepanned and I don't know what-all, they took five ounces of blood off your brain. It was an awful thing that Burl did to you, banging you with the gun."

"Oh yeah. What happened to him?"

"Got cremated, was all."

"You mean he's dead?"

"I mean I killed him."

"You had the ice pick under that napkin?"

"I did, and I stuck him with it, but only got it half in. I was beating on it, to hammer it the rest of the way, and he was battling me, trying to pull it out. I won, though. The autopsy showed it entered his heart. And your mother, she ordered the cremation job, ashes to be scattered, 'so no trace of him remains on the face of this earth,' as she said."

"He's no loss."

"You can say that again."

We spent the morning checking things back, so I got kind of caught up—beginning with the wire, that came to where she was staying, at the Truckee Motel in Reno, that Burl got the address of by pretending to be the Post Office, calling her mother to ask. "Like I said," she explained, "left me all jittered and shook, but instantly, when I saw him dead on the floor, I knew we'd made our fresh start, so don't worry about that *inny* more."

I said I wouldn't, and she told how she called the police, "knowing the number, thanks to you." She said I was still tied when they got there, "as I couldn't loosen the knots in the towels he'd tied you up with, on account of how he had wet them." It seemed she'd been held, a few minutes, till they checked her story out, but then they hustled her off to the hospital, in the same ambulance they called for me.

But in the middle of her telling about it, the door opened and there were the Langs, both on their lunch hour. And Mr. Lang you would hardly have known. From the meek, hangdog guy of the last few weeks, he was completely different, with his shoulders thrown back, his head up, and a smiling look in his eye.

"Well, well, well!" he burst out, after shaking hands with me. "I guess we found out, didn't we? Whose number was up? Who was on that hook? I'm so proud of her I could dance the Sailor's Hornpipe."

"Look," she cut in. "I can do without stuff that's going to make me seasick. I'm not proud at all, in inny way, shape, or form. If it had to be done it had to be, but let's us not talk about it."

"Okay, but *I'm* proud. See?"

"Louis, that'll do," said Mrs. Lang.

But it cleared the air, and the rest of their visit was mostly pleasant, but he kept talking about "that stuff in the papers," and how people felt about it. "It was in there about the rape," he said, "but nobody seems to mind. Now that she killed him, that makes it okay."

"Oh, how wonderful," said Sonya.

They left, finally, and then I asked her about the papers, which until then I hadn't thought about. "I saved them for you," she said, kind of grim.

She disappeared, then came back with a whole stack, the *Washington Post,* the *Washington Star,* the *Prince Georges Post,* the *Prince Georges Sentinel,* and maybe one or two others. And there it was, smeared all over the *Washington Post*:

Burwell Stuart
Stabbed to Death;
Sister-in-Law Held

There were columns about it, and also about Dale Morgan, the peculiar way she had died, and the insurance money Burl collected – even a lot about Jane, and the will she had drawn in his favor and then revoked. All kinds of stuff was there, true as far as it went, but leaving out most of what mattered, at least as I thought, reading it.

It turned out she thought so too. She said: "Gramie, if you're stuck with it, if you *have* to stay here for those tests, couldn't you put the time to some use? I mean, let Helen Musick bring the recorder, the tape recorder you have, and then dictate how it was, the true account of what happened, so it goes together to make some sense, 'stead of this mixed-up account in the papers. Then she could transcribe it for you, and who knows? Some paper might print it, just so the truth gets told."

"Yeah, well, maybe I'll give it a whirl."

So that's what I'm doing now—of course one or two names have been changed, as they used to say on *Dragnet,* "to protect the innocent"—but not many, and none of the main ones.

The tests went on, all favorable, and then one day, while Mother was there with Sonya, the door opened, and who should come in but Jane. She was in black too, but barely glanced at me. She went straight to Sonya, sat down beside her, and took her hand. "I just wanted to say," she whispered, "I know now you were telling the truth." Then she came over, picked up my hand and patted it, and took a chair that Sonya brought for her, from the hall.

"Jane," said Mother, "something occurs to me. If you'd stop trying to be the *femme fatale* of the Senior Citizen set, if you'd be your age, and deed that land to Gramie, so he can start his development now, taking you in as a partner, you'd be living, when he remodels it, in the prettiest house in the county, in the middle of the swankiest suburb, and have more money to spend than you ever had in your life. All it needs is that you stop being a goof."

"Yes, Edith, I already have."

"You already have—*what?*"

"Had the papers drawn—I couldn't sign them, however, until. . .until. . . ."

She stopped and Mother seemed annoyed. "Until. . .?" she snapped. "What are you talking about?"

"Till she knew he wouldn't die," said Sonya.

"Yes, Edith—I couldn't be sure."

She came over, put her hand on my head, which was

big from the bandages on it, said: "My little boy"—and kissed me.

That night, when Mother had gone and Jane had gone and Helen Musick had gone and the Langs had gone, Sonya leaned down to me. "I haven't told you yet," she whispered, "about me and the room they gave me—it's really a little office, but they put a cot in I can sleep on. And now you've passed your tests, now you've proved you can walk, you've also proved something else—you can play hookey if you try. My place is two doors down the hall, and I can have a nice cloud moved in, all scrubbed up and pink. And soon as the night nurse leaves, if you'd slip out in the hall and slip into my little room, there'd be someone waiting for you, and you could lie on the cloud with her, admiring the beautiful view, of moonlight and shells and cotton, in balls like little rabbits—— "

The night nurse just left.

Afterword

In 1948, James M. Cain, at 56, was, without any doubt, the most famous author in the country: he had just published two best-selling novels, *Past All Dishonor* and *The Butterfly;* paperback editions of his earlier bestsellers (*The Postman Always Rings Twice, Double Indemnity, Serenade* and *Mildred Pierce*) were still selling hundreds of thousands of copies every year, and no wonder: his themes included adultery, murder, prostitution, latent homosexuality and incest. Despite this, Paramount, Warner Bros. and MGM had finally succeeded in producing scripts that passed the Hays Office for three big movies based on Cain's novels which revived, enhanced or gave new directions to the careers of nearly a dozen actors and actresses: "Double Indemnity," 1944 (Fred MacMurray, Barbara Stanwyck and Edward G. Robinson), "Mildred Pierce," 1945 (Joan Crawford, who won an Academy Award for her performance as Mildred, Zachary Scott, Jack Carson, Eve Arden and Ann Blyth), and "The Postman," 1946 (Lana Turner, John Garfield and Hume Cronyn). In addition, he had spent most of 1947 in a running battle with both the New York Literary Establishment and the Hollywood Studios, attempting to establish his controversial American Authors Authority, which would have created a national writers' union. And in 1948, he had been involved in the Screenwriters Guild's successful efforts to remove the Communists from their entrenched position in the Guild. His name, of course, constantly turned up in the Hollywood and national gossip columns, in part because of his literary notoriety but also because of a messy divorce from his second wife, Elina Tysencka, marriage to the ex-silent movie star Aileen Pringle, a divorce from her a year later and then marriage to the former opera star Florence Macbeth. He also consumed his share of alcohol, but the big movies based on his novels had made him "hot," as Cain put it, in Hollywood, and, after an otherwise unsuccessful scriptwriting career, he could still command $2,500 a week when he took an assignment to work on a film.

Then, abruptly, Cain left Hollywood, "for no apparent reason," as Harlan Ellison wrote in his Introduction to *Hard Cain,* a collection of Cain's short novels. And to this day, veteran Hollywood hands still ask: whatever happened to James M. Cain? He was an ex-New York newspaperman and failed screenwriter who had come out of obscurity in 1934 with the publication of *The Postman,* and now, suddenly, he faded into obscurity again. Why?

What happened to James M. Cain after he reached the pinnacle of fame in 1948 is rooted in the two most important things in Cain's life—a novel and a woman. The novel was written after World War II, when suddenly Cain discovered that editors and studio heads were no longer interested in the typical Cain stories of lust, murder and corruption, which tended to paint America in unflattering colors at a time when the desired hues were red, white and blue. Frustrated and irritated, Cain decided to try a period novel, and the result was his story of a young ex-Confederate spy who falls in love with, and is loved by, a Virginia City prostitute who can, for $10, be had by any man in town—except our hero. *Past All Dishonor* was Cain's biggest hardcover success, selling 55,000 copies and bringing him praise from the critics, who applauded his fictional approach to American history. At a time when *Gone With the Wind* was the model for historical fiction, many people encouraged Cain to write more stories about the Old South and the West; "the period needs the sort of realistic treatment you can give it," one writer told him. His old friend from the *World,* the historian Alan Nevins, also chimed in, urging him to write a historical war novel. "You have all the gifts and you could be both fascinating and convincing," Nevins wrote Cain.

Cain had always been something of a Civil War buff, and his success with *Past All Dishonor*—and the financial success of *Gone With the Wind,* which had only recently been made into one of Hollywood's most celebrated movies—started Cain thinking about his own approach to the Civil War, not just a novel, but a trilogy of novels. It would be about a subject Margaret Mitchell had avoided—the cotton industry, or just how Rhett Butler made his money. But the story would be told, of course, James M. Cain style, "a romantic tale, full of skullduggeries involving large sums of money," he wrote his publisher. Cain had started researching his novels, but it quickly became apparent that he would have to go South and eventually to the Library of Congress to finish his research.

The other factor in Cain's decision to leave Hollywood was Florence Macbeth, the opera star who had been one of the divinities of his youth but whom he had never met before he was introduced to her at a Hollywood cocktail party. Cain had just separated from Aileen Pringle, and Florence was a widow who had not been in good health since the death of her husband a few years earlier. Both were middle-aged and lonely; "two cuckoos nesting in autumn," was Florence's description of the middle-aged lovers. Soon they were married, and naturally Cain discussed his urge to leave screenwriting and work on more serious books. "Either I'm going to wind up a picture writer or I'm going to get back to novels and amount to something," he told Florence. Florence, who did not like California, encouraged him to concentrate on his novels, which helped him arrive at the most important decision of his life: to shift from a newspaperman and screenwriter who also wrote novels, to "a plain 100 per cent novelist."

To pursue this goal, Cain and Florence uprooted and left California to go back East to research his story of the Civil War. They traveled for a while in the South, with Cain visiting libraries and newspapers where he took endless notes on his 3 × 5 cards. They finally settled in Hyattsville in Prince Georges County, Maryland (the setting of *Cloud Nine*), on the outskirts of Washington, D.C., where Cain wanted to continue his Civil War research in the Library of Congress. And it was a decision Cain regretted the rest of his life. California, Cain said, was "El Dorado, the Land of the Golden Promise. But I don't know anyone who is holding his breath over Prince Georges County."

Cain had originally planned a three-part saga of the Civil War, and "it must have been a saga," he wrote one editor, "because it sagged all over the place." Now he decided to focus on one book, and he wrote three drafts, "each one worse than the other," he said. "It just lay there in pieces and I did not know why." Cain was nearly sixty when he finished his Civil War research, and they began to have second thoughts about staying in Hyattsville. He wrote one friend that the move to Maryland had been a "God-awful wrench" and that neither of them accepted "this dreadful little state." At the same time, he wrote H. N. Swanson, his Hollywood agent, that one thing was certain: "In this neck of the woods . . . I don't fit in at all." He also asked Swanson if he would watch out for a job. But he heard nothing from Swanson.

So Cain settled down to work on his Civil War novel, and by 1952 he told his sister that he had written enough on the Civil War to fill ten normal books and that he had "been tempted more than once to call this one off and start another." But he also thought this was "a frightening thing to do" because any writer who does it is "an ex-writer"—and that was the one thing James M. Cain feared the most.

Meanwhile, his financial situation began to deteriorate as his savings account dwindled and the paperback royalties he had counted on to support his "serious" writing began to dry up. So he shifted to the contemporary scene and began the first of a series of novels set in Southern Maryland, hoping to recapture the magic he had discovered in Southern California. The first effort was called *Galatea,* which publisher Alfred A. Knopf liked but insisted he re-write, which took Cain much longer than he thought it would because he began to have real trouble at the typewriter—sluggish memory, fumbling for names, typos, twisted letters, confusion, inability to "unkink a story," and, worst of all, not caring "whether guy got doll or not." He finally finished *Galatea,* and when it came out in 1953 the critics were unmerciful, giving Cain, the master of the clearest, leanest literary style in America, the unkindest cut of all: his prose was dull and confusing. Saul Pett, in an AP review, said he had read all 242 pages in *Galatea* sometimes two and three times and "I still don't know quite what Cain is talking about." The book was a literary and commercial failure, although it did sell to paperback.

Cain was now fully aware that his writing powers were dwindling, and the resulting depression was not helped by the fact that even *Manhunt* magazine rejected him, turning down three stories because they were fuzzy in style and confusing. The editor—a Cain admirer—was worried about the author. So was the author. Undaunted, Cain went back to his Civil War novel, which he now called *Mignon,* that tragically took him three more years to finish. "God deliver me from a period book," he wrote William Kashland at Knopf. "But I know no way to finish them but to finish them"—and he did. In 1957, he finally sent it off to Knopf, only to receive the most crushing blow of his life: Knopf rejected it, encouraging him to re-write. This took him, believe it or not, another three years.

When Knopf rejected *Mignon* in 1957, Cain was 66, Florence's health was declining and his income was starting down again. Then, one bright spot: in the spring of 1959, he read about cholesterol in a *Newsweek* article. His doctor put him on a no-eggs, no-butter, no-fat diet, and within 48 hours he said he felt like his old self again. But he could still not hide the fact that he was growing old. "My God, he had aged so terribly," said a friend who had last seen him in California. A Hollywood radio station wrote, requesting an interview for a program it called "Living Legends." And after a lunch with Marquis Childs, who was writing an introduction to a book about Cain's old friend and boss on the *World,* Walter Lippmann (celebrating his seventieth birthday), Childs wrote: "The *World* was a constellation of men, witty, brilliant, sometimes even searching and profound. Their names, Rollin Kirby, Heywood Broun, Arthur Krock, James M. Cain, Franklin P. Adams, and many others, evoke a time that today seems more distant than the stone age."

Cain did not feel that he was a relic from the stone age or a living legend, but he could not deny that he was bogged down in the Civil War. With his new diet, however, he felt good at the typewriter again, writing Katherine White at the *New Yorker* that he was "getting more brains" than he had had in a long time. Now the writing went better, and he finished *Mignon* at the end of 1960. Then, another crushing blow: Knopf turned it down again! But this time Cain would not re-write it. Instead, he instructed his agent to find another publisher, which he did. Richard Baron at Dial bought it and assigned Jim Silberman as the editor. When it was finally scheduled for publication (in 1962), Cain wrote friends that he would soon be in the money, "on sugar hill."

If *Mignon* were just another novel, it would have been considered a success. It received moderately good reviews, sold 15,000 copies and was bought for paperback reprint. But it did not put him on Sugar Hill, one reason being that, unlike his novels of the 1930s and '40s, *Mignon* never sold to the movies.

Mignon's failure after twelve years of work was a monumental landmark in Cain's life, a crushing defeat that he never did quite understand. "Just a lotta goddamn research," he said bitterly—and, ironically, very little of the years of research Cain put into *Mignon,* or any real sense of feel of the Civil War, showed up in the slim little 246-page book. "All that reading and labor," Cain told a *New York Times* interviewer, "and a kind of mouse is born."

But Cain refused to think he was an ex-writer, and by the time *Mignon* was published in 1962 he was more than a hundred pages into a Maryland version of *Mildred Pierce*—about a woman buyer for a big Maryland department store "who attempts, through her daughter, to gain the place in the sun she herself has never attained to, an ominous creature." This new novel went through several re-writes before it was eventually published in 1965 as *The Magician's Wife.* And, despite the fact that it contained some of Cain's best writing and not one confusing, unclear page, it was another literary and commercial failure.

Although Cain would not have conceded it, the thumbs-down *The Magician's Wife* received from its critics was the final verdict on his effort to "amount to something," which had brought him East seventeen years earlier. But the truth is, as far as the only critic he paid any attention to—"Old

Man Posterity"—was concerned, Cain had already amounted to quite a bit. He wrote six books that go right on being read and re-read and made into movies. And the ironic twist to his unusual career is that *all* the stories on which his lasting reputation is based were written *before* he decided to leave California and become a serious writer.

The failure of *The Magician's Wife,* of course, did not keep Cain from his typewriter. Nothing could do that for long. He started a new novel—about a little girl who is given a tiger to raise as a pet—and wrote one friend: "Life isn't so dull exactly, but it begins to resemble a bowl of cherries that stay green all the time and resemble typewriter keys. Books, with me take longer and longer and no doubt one day will take really long." But, he wrote another, "I don't get sick, I don't fall down, I don't do much of anything, except get one day older every 24 hours. Every so often, by a process unexplained, I get out a book."

Cain was now in remarkably good health. But Florence was visibly weakening. And then on the morning of May 5, 1966, Cain tiptoed into Florence's room and found her dead. "A shock I'll never forget," he said.

Now he was alone, 75 years old and just possibly an ex-writer. The future did not look promising. But Cain was ready to face it—at his usual command post, the typewriter. He finally finished his novel about the little girl and her pet tiger, which he called *Jinghis Quinn,* and was very excited about it because of the recent success of *Born Free.* But two publishers turned it down, and Cain was a little taken aback; "I thought a law had been passed that when I wrote a book it sold," he told a friend. Undaunted, he started another one, and he wrote one friend that "Suburbia, where I live, begins to cast its spell . . . I'm beginning to realize it's the new frontier."

But James M. Cain in the Maryland suburbs was, sadly, not the same James M. Cain the literary world knew from California. He had to keep writing, however, or, as he told a friend: "I'm just a has been, a senior citizen waiting for the clock to strike. I don't mind the clock, but waiting for it and doing nothing else, terrifies me."

His next novel was about a suburban Maryland real estate developer and a teen-aged girl, and now, in addition to the frontiers of new suburbia, he decided to explore another area unfamiliar to James M. Cain—the happy ending. He had decided that happy endings were tougher, he wrote one friend, and, therefore, a "greater challenge." The result was *Cloud Nine,* and you can judge for yourself how well Cain did on his new frontier with a happy ending.

I have taken some space to go into the period of Cain's life that produced *Cloud Nine* (which was also rejected by his publisher when he wrote it in the late 1960s), but I thought it was necessary to fully understand the novel. It certainly is quintessential Cain—a "pure novel," as David Madden says in his study of Cain's fiction, one which, "more than anything else, moves even the serious reader to almost complete emotional commitment to the traumatic experience Cain renders."

After Madden said Cain wrote the "pure novel," Cain wrote him saying if by pure novel he meant one "whose point is developed from the narrative itself, rather than from some commentary on the social theme or morality of the characters, or economic or political aesthetic preachment, if that is what you mean, you hit my objective directly..."

The economic and social preachment which was at the root of *Cloud Nine* was expressed in a letter to one publisher, suggesting a promotional campaign for the novel:

"I've lived half my life," he said, "in the midst of real estate booms—first in California...and now in Southern Maryland. . . . Between climate, the overflow from Washington, D.C., and boom-feeds-upon-boom, it has a veritable madhouse of swank suburbs, jerry-built developments, and high-rise elysiums; of sewage, water, and gas problems; of politics, the good old-fashioned kind; of no-limit, blue-chip games, with millions riding the vote of Mr. Commissioner on some rezoning application. But behind this new, glittering world, I keep seeing the old Southern Maryland, as it was in the early teens, as I lived in it a while, as a young road-builder just out of college. Then it was poor, backward, and still numb from the slave economy that had riled it for hundreds of years, a world of runt corn, scrub tobacco, and tired land; of ox carts, dirt roads, and bucket wells, of saloons, gambling, blood feuds, and dark, clandestine sex. So in this story, I have attempted the counterpoint between the new and the old: the Realtor, bluff, successful, and modern, who nevertheless marries, for the honor of the family, the girl his brother got pregnant; the pretty, gray-haired widow, set in her ways, who clings to the family farm, starving to death on it, and refusing to swim with the tide that would make her rich . . . and the young girl, passionately idealistic, who nevertheless has in her bloodstream the compulsion that brings on a bloody, brutal finish. If I succeeded I don't know. I do know the story is there."

Cloud Nine also contains other essential Cain traits: the necessity to pretend to be someone else when he told his story and the ability to keep the reader turning pages, anxious to find out what happens, but always dreading the ending because of the horror you sensed would be waiting —"the wish that comes true" that Cain said most of his novels were about. But *Cloud Nine,* as any Cain fan knows, is different from the classic Cain tale: the narrator is not one of "those wonderful, seedy, lousy no-goods that you have always understood," as one of his friends described the kind of people she was urging him to return to when he was struggling with his novels late in his life; the setting is not California; and the wish that comes true does not contain the terror one expects to find at the end of a Cain story.

No one knew better than James M. Cain that he was never able to find the same spark in the suburbs of Washington and Baltimore that he found in the suburbs of Los Angeles. But the important thing is that he never stopped trying. He did not sit around waiting for the clock to strike. And he thought he had given *Cloud Nine* "the best lick I had," as he wrote his agent, and that "it held on suspense and delivered a nice wallop."

Frankly, the wallop at the end is something less than pure Cain. But the suspense does hold, and the prose reads well, like it was written by a 75-year-old James M. Cain — which it was.

As he said to one critic of his last novels: "I have to write as I write, I can't young it up."

Roy Hoopes